PROXIMA CENTAURI b
The Alien Mind

ANTHONY FUCILLA

Cover Design: Gary Pope
Editor: Vicky Sheppard

Published 2025 by arima publishing

www.arimapublishing.com

ISBN 978 1 84549 849 8

© Anthony Fucilla 2025

Swirl is an imprint of arima publishing.

arima publishing
Eagle House, Sudbury Road
Great Whelnetham
Bury St Edmunds
Suffolk, IP30 0UN
t: (+44) 01284 717884

www.arimapublishing.com

Astronomy is the oldest of the sciences.
Since time in memorial Man has looked up at the
starry skies and tried to unravel their secrets...

PROXIMA CENTAURI b THE ALIEN MIND

He was asleep, free from the domination of time but inevitably his body jerked and slowly he awoke in his dimly lit bedroom compartment. Captain John Shackleton glanced around as the nuclear fusion spacecraft thundered through the vast darkness of interstellar space. It was a first-class spacecraft named Humanitas - Alpha Centauri. It was heading to the planet Proxima Centauri b, which was located in the Alpha Centauri system 4.24 light years away. The spacecraft had virtual reality theatres, medical facilities and so much more to ensure that all the crew members were well entertained and provided for.

The spacecraft had originally launched from high-earth orbit firing up its nuclear fusion drive. It took fifteen days to accelerate under 1 g. to reach the cruising speed of 4.24 percent the speed of light. Using its nuclear fusion engine it took under two hours to pass the Moon and 14 days to pass the orbit of Mars. It was heading downwards 2.10 degrees below the ecliptic plane of the solar system. Earth and other planets went around the Sun almost like a flat disk. The star-system of Proxima Centauri b was below this disk, thus the spacecraft was on a downward flight path.

Thrusters on the outside of the spacecraft fired up causing the outer ring, with a diameter of 750 meters, to rotate and spin. To generate 1 g. of artificial gravity it needed to spin at 1.90rpm (rotations per min). After reaching 1 g. the same as on earth, the spin thrusters turned off and the spacecraft habitat ring kept spinning for the rest of the trip. This was due to the conservation of angular momentum in space. The habitat ring rotated around the hollow core of the spacecraft. This hollow core which had no gravity because it was not spinning was used for cargo storage including the space shuttles that would be used to land on the alien planet. Tracking sensors and lasers were used to deflect larger micro-meteorites, changing their trajectory away from the oncoming spacecraft and clearing a path.

Captain Shackleton rose from his small bed and stood up in the pseudo-gravity field of the spacecraft. He stretched and rubbed his bloated eyes. Within a short period he would have to return to the Command Deck. Via audio command the small vision-set sprang into life. He caught the words from an old science-fiction movie, "We're building the spacecrafts out in space beyond Saturn, where the sun's gravitational gradient is almost flat and it needs little thrust to send them right out of the solar system."

He smiled as his mind bounced and leapt back to the mission - Proxima Centauri b, that habitable planet orbiting Earth's nearest stellar neighbour, 4.24 light years away.

History beckoned. This was humanity's first voyage beyond the solar system, a leap into the unknown. But meticulous mathematical planning ensured a path had been plotted to avoid any asteroids. Not to mention that the front of the spacecraft had been built with reinforced layers. This was to prevent erosion caused by interstellar dust and gas clouds. He and the other crew members, a total of fifty, would soon arrive on Proxima Centauri b, a journey that would have taken one-hundred-years travelling at a rate of 4.24 percent the speed of light had it not been for the wormhole. Due to the wormhole, the long one-hundred-year journey had been cut down to only a matter of four years. Everything had been pre-planned. As they reached a certain point in space they entered the wormhole, a shortcut through space and time. It allowed the nuclear fusion spacecraft, which was in fact travelling at a rate of 4.24 percent the speed of light, to travel from one point of the universe to another almost instantaneously.

Had it not been for this wormhole providing a short cut through space and time, the whole mission would have been vastly different and far more complex due to the one-hundred-year trip. It would have required around 1,700 people to have boarded the flight... the cycle of life, crew members dying, babies being born, the preservation of life... a new generation of humans... There would have been strict reproduction guidelines. There would have been rules regarding family size to ensure each family had the same genetic influence on future generations and to avoid reducing genetic diversity. Each set of parents would have had to have a similar number of offspring. The number would have been set at a minimum of two and a maximum of three babies. This would have been needed in order to maintain the replacement rate of the parents and at the same time avoid high population growth that would have strained onboard resources. In addition, parents would have had to reproduce at different intervals to prevent age clusters of children. All these rules would have had to have been put in place to avoid the collapse of the passenger population. And when it was time to reproduce couples would have needed genetic counselling. Their genomes would have been sequenced to determine genetic compatibility and to understand any potential risks. Had there been any issues there would have been alternative options on board such as the artificial womb-lab or using cryogenically frozen spermatozoa and egg samples brought from earth. Having a highly genetically diverse population to start with would have made it easier to maintain that diversity over the one-hundred-year journey and beyond. Furthermore, it would have required schools, gardens, and multi-level vertical farms. Also biologists would have had to keep track of the evolution of bacteria on board the spacecraft to prevent the collapse of the ship's biosphere as the bacteria would have evolved in a closed loop system.

In terms of the journey, at the sixty-year point, the Command Deck would have initiated the gravity evolution spin sequence. Since the gravity on Proxima Centauri b is slightly higher than on earth the spin thrusters would have been periodically fired up over the next thirty years to slowly increase the spin of the habitat ring, increasing the gravity on the spacecraft so that for the last ten years of the journey the passengers - the new generation of humans would be used to living under the heavy gravity that they would soon face on their new home planet. As the gravity slowly increased on the spacecraft over the next thirty years, the lighting would have also been adjusted. The lights on the spacecraft would have slowly turned to red and dimmed to match the dark red light seen from the new sun when living on the new planet. Fifteen days before arrival the spin thrusters would have fired up again, this time in the opposite direction, to stop the spin. Then the spacecraft would have performed a flip manoeuvre so that the engines would be pointing towards Proxima Centauri b. When the engines fired up this would be the deacceleration burn to reduce velocity over the course of fifteen days at 1 g. It would slow the spacecraft down - deaccelerating in order to enter the orbit of the new planet.

Captain John Shackleton now picked up his mini pad, the glare of the light shining across his face. He read the data. It was information about time dilation; something that still interested him immensely despite his extensive knowledge on the subject. Hypothetically speaking had they been travelling for 10 years on the spacecraft, down on earth, 10 years and 3 days would have passed. This difference would have only grown larger as the spacecraft kept travelling at 4.24 percent the speed of light for the next 90 years. But due to the wormhole, the long one-hundred-year journey had been astonishingly reduced to only a matter of four years. Furthermore if one-hundred-years had passed on the spacecraft, one-hundred-years and thirty-three days would have passed on earth. Then a message would have been sent out from the spacecraft to earth announcing the historic arrival. The message would have taken 4.24 years to reach earth and another 4.24 years for the spacecraft to receive a reply - a total of 8.48 years. Thus the spacecraft would be communicating into the past.

He placed the mini pad on the small bed and walked over to the window and there caught sight of the new host Sun... Proxima Centauri, the Red Dwarf. It was distinct but faint. Its brightness was much lower than that of Earth's Sun. It would have taken fifty years, the halfway point of the one-hundred-year journey, for anyone to have had their first glimpse of the new host star but thanks to the wormhole it had taken them only two years, the halfway point of the four year journey. He suddenly began to think.... 'The new sun will appear larger in the sky and the light will have a reddish colour. At 65 percent the brightness, I and the other crew members, including the future colonists on Proxima Centauri b will be living with a lower light level equivalent to early evening on Earth.' He then recalled a specific lecture four months before the journey...

"Proxima Centauri b... Well, in a world with less light and a red hue, human eyes will adapt and evolve in several ways: the iris could turn a shade of amber or gold to optimise for the red light. Pupils could be larger to allow more light in making the eyes look darker overall. The white part of the eye could become more pigmented to reduce glare and improve vision in the dim light."

He snapped out of his thought drenched daze. It was time to return to the Command Deck and eventually he and the others would be taking their small shuttles, which were stored inside the hollow core of the spacecraft, down to the new planet to see for themselves.

The small space shuttle shuddered and tipped in the turbulent alien sky. Finally it landed on Proxima Centauri b. The other shuttles would soon follow and make their landings too. The mother spacecraft remained in orbit piloted by machines, AI, high-tech supercomputers. The airlock hissed open and Captain Shackleton and several crew members stepped out onto alien soil, their boots sinking into the reddish-brown dust, pressure suits and oxygen masks fitted tightly. They were finally there... Humanity's first voyage beyond the solar system was successful. They were now in a totally different region of the galaxy. They all felt the slightly higher gravity of the planet as they gazed in awe, firstly at the alien landscape and then at the shining red dwarf star, Proxima.

The planet Proxima Centauri b was tidally locked to its star. One side of the planet always faced the red dwarf star experiencing perpetual daylight, while the other side was in constant darkness. It lacked a day/night cycle. It was a world of extremes, its day side marked by intense radiation from its red dwarf star and its night side locked in icy darkness. They were going to set up a base and live on the side of the planet that always faced its star but living on a planet that didn't have a day/night cycle like Earth was going to take some getting used to. Regardless, it held the promise of a new beginning for the human race. Terraforming drones would soon be put to work to convert the thin toxic atmosphere into something breathable.

The settlers quickly established their base with domed habitats and research stations. Over time they began to explore the alien planet, their new home, with a desire to unravel all its mysteries. They soon discovered vast underground caves filled with strange bioluminescent fungi, hinting at a complex ecosystem below the surface. These wonderful discoveries raised more questions. Could Proxima b support life? As they delved deeper they discovered cryptic symbols and carvings that suggested an advanced long lost alien civilisation. Captain Shackleton and the others were filled with both excitement and trepidation. The news soon spread amongst the settlers. Were they alone in this distant corner of the galaxy, or were they trespassers on a world that once belonged to others? This new alien world was a treasure trove of mysteries waiting to be unravelled.

John sat inside an oxygen-controlled, thick domed habitat. Machines bleeped and chimed. Due to the unending daylight, sleep cycles had been affected. The dome itself was cluttered with grey-box science and computer gear. The interior was brilliantly clean and there was no need for artificial light. The unending light shed from the red dwarf star Proxima was more than enough.

In his hand he held a small remote. He wanted to see if it still worked. He pressed the button. With a whir of servos the back of his bed began to tip up. "It's working perfectly," he muttered. Placing the small remote down he picked up an old book, the only thing that reminded him of home... Earth. It was the only book that he had brought with him. He began to read...

'The story of the universe is written in light. Light carries the hidden truths of reality. Yet as we have come to understand its nature, light has revealed something far more profound: the existence of unseen dimensions that stretch beyond our conventional understanding of space and time. Light is an electromagnetic wave... a disturbance that travels through space, oscillating between electric and magnetic fields. Light is the messenger that reveals the curvature and structure of space-time itself. The laws of gravity and electromagnetism, which appear so different in our three-dimensional world, are two aspects of the same phenomenon when viewed from a higher-dimensional perspective. Just as a two-dimensional being cannot fully understand a three-dimensional object, we, as three-dimensional creatures, could not perceive the true nature of light without considering the fifth dimension.'

He shrugged and began flicking through the pages and found another chapter. He read...

'Could consciousness itself be a fundamental aspect of the universe, woven into the symphony of space and time? The universe may not be a passive system but a dynamic collaboration between matter, energy, and observers. The Quantum Mind: Advanced theories propose that consciousness arises from quantum processes in the brain, connecting us to the quantum fabric of reality. In this view, we are not merely spectators but participants in the universal symphony – beings whose awareness gives meaning to the cosmic design.'

He placed the book on the small plastic translucent table next to the bed and stood up. He decided it was time to do some more exploring, but he would need to be dressed accordingly with his pressure suit and oxygen-mask placed safely on, after all, he was in the Alpha Centauri system where Earth time and calendars were completely irrelevant. In terms of astronomical distances, he was a long way from home... a mind-blowing distance. But it was all relative of course. A distance of around four light years wasn't much on the scale of the volume of space that contained the thousands of stars visible to the human eye.

After a long walk dressed in his pressure suit John reached the mouth of a cave and there he halted breathing in controlled oxygen. Inside his head there were moments when John felt overwhelmed by a kind of black depression, but he had to control it, after all, he was the captain. He rubbed the face of his mask with his gloved hand under the unending daylight... 'It's going to take some time for me and the others to adjust to the slightly heavier gravity here... The nerve receptors that handle my posture, positioning and movement are all baffled right now...' he mused to himself. Proxima Centauri b's surface gravity was higher than Earth's due to its higher mass and higher density. In an effort to get his bearings, he looked up into the alien sky and glanced at the red dwarf. Proxima flared almost constantly, like all red dwarf stars, making explosive releases of magnetic energy that were visible across light years. Most of Proxima Centauri b's atmosphere had been stripped away by radiation from its star. The planet encountered bouts of extreme ultraviolet radiation. 'No plant from Earth could flourish here,' he thought. On Earth, humans lived in a kind of sea of other organisms, including the bacteria that lived inside and outside their own bodies. All life on Earth is based on two chemicals, two acids: DNA, which stores the information that defines a life form, and RNA, which interprets that information and uses it to assemble proteins... the very building blocks of life... DNA as software, proteins as hardware...

Shielding his eyes with his gloved hand John looked straight up at Proxima, at the huge spots that crowded its face, localised flares showing like scars then he turned and entered the cave. He instantly caught sight of a brilliant ball of fiery light. His mind returned to the opening line of his book. 'The story of the universe is written in light. Light carries the hidden truths of reality.'

'How strange and ironic that I should be seeing this, given what I have just read,' he thought at first, but as he continued to observe it his eyes grew wide with fear as he registered a faint hum and an eerie energy emanating from the source. Even so, despite the fear that suddenly gripped him, a certain fascination suddenly took hold of him. Carefully he inched over towards the brilliant ball of fiery light. It hovered, pulsed and glowed.

"What the heck is this?" he muttered to himself analytically trying to absorb the physical reality of it. Suddenly like a lightning bolt a blinding beam of light projected out heading in his direction. It hit his facemask penetrating through. He shook violently as if electrocuted and then dropped to the hard ground like a dead man, eyes open wide... oxygen-mask intact.

TIME elapsed...

"Man from Proxima is what they call him," remarked explorer, paranormal investigator and freelance journalist Roman Nebraska. He raised an enquiring eyebrow at his colleague, Susan Schumacher, who sat across from him as he casually sat on his chair swinging his legs up so that his feet rested on the desk.

"Yes, the Man from Proxima who was found in a cave... up there!" she replied merrily, her blue eyes sparkling.

Roman cracked his knuckles and said, "When the settlers, the other crew members, found him in that cave they initially thought he was dead. Strangely enough according to reports his eyes were wide open, staring as if mad but not responsive in any way at all. Apparently he's been like that ever since. Eyes wide open and yet disconnected from the world, unable to speak or communicate at any level. How strange! Who knows what took place up there? I'd love to know. Since his return to Earth he has remained in that private government funded hospital getting the best care. He's been well looked after by a team of elite doctors, that's for sure but who knows if he will ever break free from his coma? I hope he will. It's crazy to think that he spent four years like that on a spacecraft travelling back to Earth through deep space and now he has spent another four years like that in a hospital here on Earth... a total of eight years."

"Well hopefully he will eventually come round, recuperate. He can't even feed himself. He's been fed intravenously ever since the ordeal, both on the spacecraft during his return home to earth and then at the hospital," said Susan.

Roman stood up and rubbed his smooth jaw in thought. "Yeah, let's hope for the best! I would certainly love to interview that man at some point... Captain John Shackleton, what a name." He paused briefly. "He's a living piece of history... one of the first men to traverse the universe travelling on a spacecraft at a rate of 4.24 percent the speed of light... destination Proxima Centauri b. It was a journey that should have taken them one-hundred-years, but thanks to that wormhole it was reduced to only four. Staggering thought... but then, so is infinity."

"I wonder how the settlers are getting on up there," asked Susan.

"Well," he replied briskly with a sudden flash of insight, "the last we, that is, the citizens of Earth, heard was that the settlers were making great progress. The terraforming project is going well with no sign of aliens, that is, none have been seen thus far. However, they did discover vast underground caves filled with strange bioluminescent fungi. They have also discovered cryptic symbols and carvings. Perhaps an advanced, long-lost alien civilisation lived there and somehow went extinct. Anyway, that's pretty much it thus far. Remember, communicating with the settlers on Proxima b is not easy. Each message takes 4.24 years to arrive here, and then another 4.24 years for them to receive a reply. A total of 8.48 years..."

Suddenly Susan checked her watch. "Gosh, talking of time, I've got to rush. I have a meeting with the boss. Almost forgot."

She stood up and walked out of the office in a hurry with her cream-coloured handbag on her shoulder and her high heels clicking against the hard floor. Stimulated by what he had shared with Susan, Roman had the urge to do some basic research pertaining to the planet Proxima b. He grabbed his Data-Pad from across his desk. He wanted some facts and figures. Sitting back down he began to read quietly... "The expected gravity on Proxima Centauri b is set to be around 1.026 times that of earth making it just slightly stronger; a person who weighs 50kg on earth will feel as if they weigh 51.4kg on Proxima Centauri b..." Roman paused for a moment. The simple arithmetic of the Earth's gravitational field blazed in his mind, as if written in letters of fire. He continued to read... "This slight added gravity means increased stress on the heart and cardiovascular system. Bones and muscles will undergo changes becoming denser to support the higher gravity. The bodies' fluids will also redistribute slightly leading to increase blood pressure in the lower limbs. Over time the human species will become shorter on average with a more compact body shape so as to be more energy efficient in the higher gravity environment."

'Fascinating,' he thought placing the Data-Pad back down on the desk. He now looked up at the large poster that was pinned to the wall, as he had done countless times before. It was a picture of Planet Earth hanging in the darkness of space. Beneath lay a quote printed in yellow. It read... 'Earth is just 1 of 3.2 trillion planets in our galaxy. The Sun is just 1 of 200 billion stars in the Milky Way. The Milky Way is just 1 of 2 trillion galaxies in the observable universe.'

Darkness had fallen over New York. But it did not drown out the chaos that enveloped the city. The smell of life was everywhere. Roman Nebraska was at home sitting on the large sofa. His house was rather large for a single man. The walls were filled with expensive paintings and there were beautiful statues placed in various rooms. He loved art and that was reflected in the house he owned. He came from an extremely wealthy, powerful family. Financially he was more than secure. He only worked as a freelance journalist because he loved to write and research, working with several newspapers and magazines. As for the office, well, it was more to break away from the boredom of working from home. In addition it was a good place to socialise and connect with the other journalists. He could go to the office when he chose at random.

During his career as a paranormal investigator he had worked on many different cases, such as individuals who claimed to communicate telepathically and others where people claimed they were reincarnated and would speak about their previous lives. He had also visited India and Sri Lanka interviewing firewalkers trying to determine the secret behind the technique. The ritual of firewalking, the act of walking barefoot over a bed of hot embers or stones, had been practised by many cultures all over the world for centuries, along with other painful religious rituals. He also interviewed people who claimed they had the power of telekinesis and could move things with their mind.

He also considered himself an explorer and had travelled extensively. He had been to Loch Ness in Scotland in search of the Loch Ness monster. As unlikely and bizarre as the story was, it still drew him there. He had also worked with a team of marine biologists and highly skilled divers on a ship out in the South Atlantic. They had claimed to have seen a great sea serpent, and he had joined the search for it. He was also fascinated by the numerous reports of giant cephalopods, both octopus and squid, as well as sharks and other amazing sea dwellers. He had also been involved with a team of eccentric anthropologists who were in search of Bigfoot. They claimed it lived in the Six Rivers National Forest located in the north-western corner of California. Shortly after he'd also had the opportunity to venture out to the Himalayas with another team of anthropologists in search of the Yeti, but due to a bout of pleurisy at the time was sadly unable to go. The Yeti, as the Nepalese called it, had been a persistent Himalayan myth. It was meant to be a dangerous monster larger than any man. But it had never been captured, photographed, or even described by reputable witnesses.

Thoughts of his ex-girlfriend Tessa suddenly interrupted his musings. Accompanied by an expression of mild discomfort... He had been with her for only one year, but to him it felt like a lifetime. The relationship ended abruptly, without explanation two months ago. It still hurt.

Somehow, whenever he thought of her, it brought to mind a vivid memory of a specific moment in time... hot sunlight filtering down on them as they walked through a green park; summer breezes stirring around them as they toiled joyfully... the air smelling of sun and grass... insects buzzing around them. One part of his brain recalled this vivid moment, while another part reminded him that it was now only a meaningless memory. He shrugged his shoulders and decided to push it aside. It was pointless dwelling on the past.

In the silence of the living-room he now began to think about Susan. She was a dynamic lady. Although the relationship was purely platonic, he admired her in so many ways. She ticked all the boxes as far as he was concerned. She was a pretty, blue-eyed brunette, smart, with a lovely personality. Her father was from Berlin, Germany and her mother was from Caracas, Venezuela. She herself was born and brought up in New York City. It was quite a dazzling mix.

He gave an audio-command to the large rectangular TV and it lit up obediently. With the remote he selected the science channel and raised the volume. It was an old documentary. Scientist and writer Aldo Santostasi was being interviewed. Roman listened with keen interest as he spoke:

"Well... one explanation of this mystery is that in fact all the other possible Universes do exist... somewhere! But of course, the vast majority are lifeless." Roman raised the volume continuing to listen chewing his lower lip thoughtfully. "Only in an infinitesimally small fraction of the total Creation are the parameters such that matter can exist, stars can form... and, ultimately, life can arise. Thus we are here because we couldn't be anywhere else."

'How interesting,' he thought, leaning forward and then flung himself back in the chair as he realised with some annoyance that the documentary was ending and he had just caught the final part. He changed the channel and across the screen could see a jumbled wasteland of craters, mountain ranges and ravines. The crests of the mountains, catching the low sun, burned like islands of fire in a sea of darkness. Again he switched over. And this time found another science documentary. It was all about Proxima and his eyes became glued to the screen. Astronomer, Anthony Canterbury was speaking:

"Alpha Centauri is a triple star system. The stars in the Alpha Centauri system include a pair called 'A' and 'B,' which orbit relatively close to each other. Alpha Centauri A is a near twin of our Sun in almost every way, including age, while Alpha Centauri B is somewhat smaller and dimmer but still quite similar to the Sun. The third member, Alpha Centauri C, also known as Proxima, is a much smaller red dwarf star that travels around the AB pair in a much larger orbit that takes it more than 10 thousand times farther from the AB pair than the Earth-Sun distance. After our Sun which is a star, Proxima Centauri is the next nearest star to Earth, 4.24 light years away.

Furthermore, Proxima Centauri is a red dwarf star with a mass of around 12.5% of the sun and a diameter of about 14% of our star's... However, Proxima Centauri is around 33 times denser than the sun, according to most astronomers. This red dwarf is a main sequence star, which means that, like the sun, it is still turning hydrogen to helium at its core via nuclear fusion, with this acting as Proxima Centauri's main source of energy. With a luminosity of 0.17% that of the sun Proxima Centauri is producing energy at a lower rate than the sun... That means that, while our star is predicted to have a main sequence lifetime of around 10 billion years, of which around 5 billion years remain, Proxima Centauri will stay on this branch of stellar evolution for another 4 trillion years — around 300 times the current 13.8-billion-year age of the universe. Although Proxima Centauri will outlive the sun, it will eventually experience a similar fate: When its supply of hydrogen is exhausted, Proxima Centauri will end its life as a smouldering white dwarf star, lacking the mass sufficient to become a neutron star or a black hole."

Roman was fascinated by what he was hearing. He continued to listen...

"Alpha Centauri A is the principal member of the binary system. It is a solar-like main-sequence star with a similar yellowish colour, whose stellar classification is spectral type G2-V; it is about 10 percent more massive than the Sun, with a radius about 22 percent larger. The type of magnetic activity on Alpha Centauri A is comparable to that of the Sun, showing coronal variability due to star spots, as modulated by the rotation of the star. Alpha Centauri B is the secondary star of the binary system. It is a main-sequence star of spectral type K1-V, making it more an orange colour than Alpha A; it has 90 percent of the mass of the Sun and a 14 percent smaller diameter.

Although it has a lower luminosity than A, Alpha Centauri B emits more energy in the X-ray band. It is more magnetically active than Alpha Centauri A…"

His curiosity satisfied, Roman again changed the channel and found another science documentary. An old man was speaking…

"The Andromeda Galaxy is the nearest major galaxy to the Milky Way. It is 2.5 million light years away from Earth. Like the Milky Way, it is a barred spiral galaxy, so-called for the bar-like structure formed by the stars in its centre. Andromeda is larger than the Milky Way in terms of the distance it extends. However, the two galaxies are roughly comparable in mass, and it's hard to say which one is more massive. When the Milky Way and Andromeda merge in about 4.5 billion years, they will probably form a huge elliptical galaxy. Chances are that our solar system will be seriously affected. We might be pulled away from the centre of the galaxy, or we might be totally ejected from it. Stars are so far apart that any sort of collision is extremely unlikely. However, it's almost certain that the increasing luminosity of our sun will have caused Earth to become inhospitable to all multicellular life by this point, so we will not be around to find out."

Suddenly the doorbell rang shattering the moment. Roman muted the volume and stood up making his way to the front door. As he opened he saw his good friend Martin McGregor standing there slender and well dressed as always. He was dark haired and chiselled. His slick light-green hover-car was parked on the road in the gloom. In the distance there was the sound of a metallic ring, an empty can striking the ground.

"An unexpected visit," chimed Roman warmly, "but a pleasant one. Come in."

Within a few minutes, they were sitting on the sofa in the main living-room, drinking rum and chatting away.

"Roman believe me, I've no words to describe the adrenaline rush you get from such an experience. Climbing Everest was simply divine. You of all people would love it. It's the ultimate experience that one could have here on Earth." Martin's eyes became distant and reflective... "By midnight, the summit of Everest was around a hundred and twenty yards away, a pyramid of snow, pale and ghostly in the light of the rising moon. The sky above was cloudless. And the wind that had been blowing for many days had dropped almost to zero."

"You should be a writer giving descriptions like that," grinned Roman.

Martin smiled and said gleefully, "Almost a year has passed since the climb, but it has forever remained embedded in my mind."

"I bet. Tell me... How's your brother Luther doing?"

"Good. He's still working as a computer programmer in the Applied Physics Division. So what about you Roman? Still getting over it?"

"Tessa, you mean?"

"Yes..."

"That's history, but I must admit, I do have my moments. I really liked her. Thought it would work out... I pictured us getting married, having kids, travelling, the whole works. But then one day she just picked up and left without explanation. Two months ago... We were together for a whole year." He grimaced. "Anyway Martin, you've heard all of this before many times now."

"Yes indeed my friend."

"Anyway, how's your love life going? Any luck?"

"Well, I've recently started dating this girl, Genevieve. Met her in a bar a couple of weeks back. Boy is she cute. She's from Lyon, France. I just love the accent, her broken English. Anyway, things are going pretty well."

"Is she the marrying type?"

"Possibly... Early days..."

"What does she do?"

"She's an art teacher. And a very talented one, indeed... I've seen some of her paintings and drawings. They look like photographs, almost as if they were AI generated. She's quite a talent."

"Does she know that you're a loaded bum with a PHD in palaeontology?"

"Well Roman, she's seen my place numerous times now, and she knows that I don't work. I spend most of my time with her telling her about my hobbies, and of course, the main one... mountain climbing. I've told her all about my experience climbing Mount Everest."

"I bet you have."

"She wants me to go to France with her. She tells me it's the most beautiful country in the world, and that the food and wine are the best." He shrugged. "So, what's happening with you? Anything new to report in the world of the paranormal...? Any new adventures planned?"

Roman rubbed his forehead and replied, "No, nothing new in the department of the paranormal at the moment. In terms of adventures, exploring, well, my last was working with a team of anthropologists who were in search of Bigfoot, as you know."

"Yes, I recall you telling me. That was your last?"

"Yes. However, shortly after the search for Bigfoot was completed, I did have the opportunity to venture out to the Himalayas with another team of anthropologists in search of the Yeti but I couldn't go due to a bout of pleurisy of all things. I never told you about that..."

"Himalayas... the Yeti!" gasped Martin. "Now that would have been an experience. As you know Mount Everest, the mountain I climbed is located in the Mahalangur Himal sub-range of the Himalayas. Spectacular scenery there... Anyway, back to Bigfoot... Bigfoot living in the Six Rivers National Forest located in the north-western corner of California..." Martin smirked and then chuckled. "What a waste of time that was... a baffled wonder. Your adventures have a kind of mad logic that makes them convincing by their very improbability."

"Martin as an adventurer, freelance journalist, and paranormal investigator even the most bizarre cases will appeal, and nothing can be taken for granted. Our planet is filled with all kinds of mystery, the paranormal. There are beasts and all kinds of creatures that science has yet to discover. Take the ocean... it is filled with the unknown. It teems with all kinds of alien-like marine creatures that are still waiting to be discovered by man. The general rule of thumb for an adventurer, explorer, like me is - nothing is impossible."

"Fair enough," said Martin. He contemplated for a brief second and continued... "Now that you mention the ocean, I must say I've always been fascinated by the sea. Jellyfish look damn scary if you ask me."

"Indeed," replied Roman. "As you know I've worked with scuba-divers and marine biologists on a ship out in the South Atlantic."

"Yes, I remember you telling me all about it. They claimed to have seen a great sea serpent, correct?"

"Yes, that's right. I personally never saw the thing during my time with them. Anyway, many of them had stories to tell concerning jellyfish... close encounters. Did you know that there are more than 2,000 species of jellyfish swimming through the world's waters? Most stings are completely harmless. Some will leave you in excruciating pain. Then there are the killers. Many of the world's deadliest jellyfish are box jellyfish, which refers to the species' cube-shaped meduae. The northern Australian box jellyfish is possibly the world's most venomous animal. Its tentacles can reach lengths of up to three meters long, while its bell is about the size of a human head."

"Ugh! Still it's fascinating stuff, Roman..."

"They also told me about their encounters with the giant squid."

"Wow... what happened?"

"Well one of the scuba-divers was actually attacked by one. Luckily he managed to break free."

"That must have been terrifying."

"For sure but these divers are fearless and very well trained. Experts, in fact... They know that it's a high-risk occupation." He paused for a moment... "Anyway, giant squid can snatch prey up to 33 feet away by shooting out their two feeding tentacles, which are tipped with hundreds of powerful sharp-toothed suckers. These feeding tentacles are very long, often doubling the total length of the giant squid on their own. Like other squid species, they have eight arms and two longer feeding tentacles that help them bring food to their beak-like mouths. Some suggest they might even attack and eat small whales."

"I've read about cephalopod attacks on humans that date back to ancient times," said Martin fully engrossed in the conversation. "Many claim that even boats and ships have been attacked by giant squids and giant octopuses."

"Yes, that's right. Fascinating things these beasts..." Roman rubbed his chin in thought, digging around his memory for more interesting facts to tantalise his friend. "Did you know that the giant squid, along with their cousin, the colossal squid, have the largest eyes in the animal kingdom, measuring some 10 inches in diameter? These massive organs allow them to detect objects in the lightless depths where other animals would see nothing." He paused in reflection and smiled. "From the research boat I recall seeing fish as dazzling as neon signs wandering around near the surface of the ocean. It seemed not only breathtakingly lovely but also a peaceful world. No haste, no sign of the struggle for existence. This of course was just an illusion. The sea world is all about brutal survival."

Martin sipped at his glass of rum, intrigued. He then asked, "Have you had any dangerous encounters with creatures from the deep?"

"No... I never went into the ocean. I remained on the vessel at all times."

"Smart. What about dangerous land creatures? Any encounters...?"

"Well during my time in Zambia, Africa, one evening, I almost stepped on a snake. Luckily I spotted it just in time and it slithered away. It was a close call."

"Really...?"

"Yes... it was the Gaboon Viper. I recognised it immediately. It happens to be a very mild-mannered snake, and rarely hisses or exhibits signs of aggression, unless stepped on or overtly provoked which is a problem because it is also a master of disguise, and blends seamlessly into its surroundings thanks to its intricate diamond-shaped pattern of browns, yellows and purples that mimic the forest floor. It's deadly, nocturnal and ranges across sub-Saharan Africa. The one I saw was a small one but they grow anywhere between 4-6 feet in length and weigh up to a staggering 25 pounds. It's the heaviest venomous snake on the continent."

"Never heard of it, but it sounds formidable," replied Martin.

"Well, if you leave it in peace you'll be okay. It preys on a variety of small to medium-sized animals."

"Interesting…"

"I mentioned its remarkable camouflage… well it relies on this to hunt, and strikes with incredible speed and precision at its unsuspecting prey. It's not the fastest striker in the snake world, but it has huge venom glands, which contribute significantly to its ability to store and deliver such large quantities of venom and can deliver a staggering 200-1000 mg of potent venom per bite delivered through what herpetologists say are the longest fangs in the snake world."

"How long are its fangs exactly…?"

"Around two inches… It's basically the longest-fanged serpent in the world. And they have to be highly retractable so it can close its mouth. I mean the combination of the camouflage, the venom and the fangs all mean its prey is subdued really quickly and it is considered to be a highly efficient predator."

"Is there antivenom for humans…?"

"Yes of course and it should be administered as soon as possible to save the affected limb or indeed the victim's life. The snake's venom is cytotoxic and cardiotoxic."

"What does its venom do to a human?"

"Well a bite from a Gaboon viper causes rapid and conspicuous swelling, intense pain, severe shock, and local blistering. Other symptoms may include uncoordinated movements, defecation, urination, swelling of the tongue and eyelids, convulsions, and unconsciousness. Blistering, bruising, and necrosis may be extensive."

"Sounds like the stuff of nightmares," Martin said, grimacing.

"Yeah and that's not the end of it; the blood may become incoagulable, with internal bleeding that may lead to haematuria and haematemesis. Local tissue damage may require surgical excision and possibly amputation to any affected limb."

"Wow... you are like a computer Roman, a walking, talking AI. Your mind is filled with so much data."

Roman smiled and said, "Thanks Martin. Experience is knowledge. Anyway, jumping away from the world of deadly creatures both at sea and on land, from a sheer journalistic perspective, I've still got my mind set on interviewing the Man from Proxima. At least I'm hoping..."

"Still...? You've got a long wait. He's been in that hospital for years... kept alive on a drip. If you want my opinion, I think he won't last too much longer. And even if he does wake up, he will probably live the rest of his life in a wheelchair or something, like a wrinkled mummy."

"We'll see," Roman replied, almost resigned to the fact that it might indeed, never happen.

"I must admit though," Martin observed, "it would be a historic interview... Wow, the Man from Proxima. He has gone down in history already, he's a legend. I bet the whole planet will want a piece of him if he snaps out of his coma. Journalists and news reporters from all over the world would come to New York in search of an interview with the legend. They would all flock here." He paused then continued... "I must say space has always fascinated me. To think that man has reached Alpha Centauri, the triple star system, is absolutely mind-blowing... And now as we speak the planet Proxima Centauri b is inhabited with humans that are terraforming the planet as it orbits around the red dwarf star Proxima Centauri. After our very own Sun, Proxima Centauri is the next nearest star to Earth... a staggering 4.24 light years away... wow." He rubbed his eyes and continued, "I remember as a kid reading a picture book all about Saturn. I loved looking at the pictures. I used to sit there for hours trying to grasp the fact that this incredible object, with its silver rings spinning around it, wasn't just some artist's dream, but actually existed. That it was a world, a planet, ten times the size of Earth. The ring system is very thin, you know... only about twenty miles in thickness. Billions of separate particles that make them up are so widely spaced. It's only when you look into the distance that the countless fragments merge into a continuous sheet."

Suddenly the vid-phone rang. Susan's face appeared across the small screen. Roman leapt to his feet, rushed over to the vid-phone and activated it with the pressing of a button. Their eyes locked.

"Roman, you haven't heard the breaking news?"

"No..."

"The Man from Proxima, Captain John Shackleton is finally awake. It's all over the news. According to news reports he's been awake for around five hours now. It didn't take long for the news to get out. Apparently he's undergoing tests as we speak."

"What? Wow! This is unbelievable news... great news, truly."

"Yes. The minute I heard I had to call you."

Roman smiled and punched the air.

"This is the moment I have been waiting for." He crowed gleefully. "Okay Susan. Thank you for letting me know, speak tomorrow."

"Sure thing..."

Roman deactivated the vid-phone, the face of Susan fading away slowly into ripples of visual static. He rushed back to the sofa and collapsed there, eyes wide. Grabbing the remote he turned facing Martin and said excitedly, "How ironic is that? We were just speaking about the legend a few minutes ago and now the breaking news."

"I know, isn't that something..." said Martin.

Roman found the news channel and raised the volume. A newsman was making a statement:

"The Man from Proxima has finally awoken after years of being in a coma. According to reports Captain John Shackleton is alert and responsive, currently undergoing tests. Stay tuned for more..."

Roman's eyes briefly locked with Martin's.

"This is the moment I've waited for my friend."

After awakening, Captain John Shackleton had spent a full month in hospital undergoing all sorts of tests, mainly ones pertaining to his brain, such as cognitive function, memory, puzzle solving and so forth. Once he was passed fit he was released and sent home. After only two days, he was bombarded with phone calls from national and international journalists, television stations, and news reporters all wanting a piece of him... the Man from Proxima. His telephone number had leaked out and gone viral. His personal assistant and long-time friend Alexanko Papadopoulos, who lived on the premises with John, dealt with all the calls and requests. All were temporarily refused and put on hold.

However, three weeks later, Roman managed to pull off the unexpected. Unlike the others, he had handwritten a polite letter and sent it directly to John. Due to his fame, everyone knew where the Man from Proxima lived, and the old-fashioned way worked. Roman had an extraordinary knack of getting his way when he found it necessary. He received a call from John's personal assistant Alexanko telling him that John had read his letter and was happy to proceed with the interview and that it was to be held at his home. When Roman asked how much it would cost to be the first man to interview him he was told that it would cost nothing. Although pleasantly surprised, he wondered why. The interview was scheduled for Monday, 1:30pm. The mansion was located on the outskirts of New York; a very wealthy lavish area.

On the morning of the interview Roman got up early, fuelled by excitement. He had told everyone about the upcoming interview with the Man from Proxima, friends and family alike. He was proud to be the first person that would interview the legend. This was going to be historic.

It was 7am and he had plenty time to kill. Sitting on the sofa he activated the TV via audio-command. Finding the science channel he sat back. 'This is the perfect way to prepare myself for the interview,' he thought. He raised the volume as a middle-aged man spoke, the ubiquitous Professor Michael Baggott.

'Earth is about 4.5 billion years old. Most scientists like me think that by 4.3 billion years ago, Earth may have developed conditions suitable to support life. The oldest known fossils, however, are only 3.7 billion years old. Life first evolved as single-celled organisms in the Archean era, then as eukaryotic-celled life in the Proterozoic era. Then in the Palaeozoic, the Mesozoic, and the Cenozoic eras, which are all marked by mass extinction events, multicellular life flourished and evolved. Earth is the right distance from the Sun, it is protected from harmful solar radiation by its magnetic field, it is kept warm by an insulating atmosphere, and it has the right chemical ingredients for life, including water and carbon. Recently some scientists have narrowed in on the hypothesis that life originated near a deep-sea hydrothermal vent. The chemicals found in these vents and the energy they provide could have fuelled many of the chemical reactions necessary for the evolution of life. Furthermore, there are so many animal life forms on Earth because of evolution and the diversity of environments on the planet. All life evolved from a single-celled organism way back... around 3 billion years ago. It evolved into so many different creatures because of a beautiful relationship between design changes, DNA mutations, and the diversity of environments offered by Earth. Biodiversity is the enormous variety of life on earth. Several species on earth are a result of evolution. Constant natural and manmade activities have changed environmental conditions. There are many different environments on earth. Each environment includes resources, food, etc, and each environment presents challenges to survival. Species adapt to their environments and become good at overcoming the challenges and consuming the resources.'

As a result of Professor Baggott's words, Roman began to think about humanity's quest to conquer space... 'How would mankind evolve and adapt on Proxima Centauri b? There were bound to be biological and neurology changes over the course of time. Earthly man subjected to an alien environment, was bound to change significantly, regardless of the terraforming project,' he thought. In his mind he replayed the final words of Professor Baggott... 'Species adapt to their environments and become good at overcoming the challenges and consuming the resources.' He sat there thinking deeply...

Would the humans on Proxima Centauri b lose their humanity overtime? What would become of them? He changed channel and the famous philosopher, writer and musicologist Mark Castleray, said elegant as ever...

'String theory, proposes that the fundamental building blocks of the universe are not particles but tiny, vibrating strings. These strings oscillate in multiple dimensions far more than the four dimensions of space-time we observe. In its most advanced form, string theory requires the existence of ten dimensions, with six of them curled up so tightly that they remain invisible to us. In this framework, the fifth dimension is no longer just a mathematical curiosity. It is a real part of the universe... one that helps unify the fundamental forces of nature.

Light, gravity, and even the strong and weak nuclear forces can all be understood as different vibrations of strings moving through higher-dimensional space. What if the universe, at its deepest level, is not made of points or particles but of vibrating strings, tiny loops of energy that resonate through the hidden dimensions of space and time? String theory has transformed our understanding of reality. It suggests that the cosmos is not just a collection of particles but a symphony of vibrations, a masterpiece of mathematics and music. If string theory is indeed correct, our universe is just one of many in a vast multiverse. The multiverse emerges as a profound and inevitable consequence of higher-dimensional geometry. Each universe might arise from strings vibrating in unique ways, producing different particles, forces, and physical laws. Furthermore, some universes might be entirely inhospitable to life. Others might host alternate forms of matter and energy.'

With echoes of the lecture from Mark Castleray in mind, Roman's thoughts returned to the interview...

Finally, Roman was on his way. The drive itself was an epic worthy of a complete story. He was as ready as he could be and his mind was split between fine-tuning his plans for the historic interview to come and the fascinating radio broadcast about how two people communicated in dreams. The radio finally claimed his full attention...

'For the first time, two people have successfully communicated in their dreams. The research demonstrated that lucid dreams could unlock new dimensions of communication and humanity's potential.'

'Wow!' he thought.

'Two individuals successfully induced lucid dreams and exchanged a simple message with specially designed equipment. A lucid dream is a phenomenon where a person knows he's dreaming while still being in a dream state. The company maintains that REM sleep allows individuals to immerse themselves in a fully developed reality where they can see, hear, touch, smell, taste, experience pleasure and pain, and even alter their body and gender. Unlike physical reality, REM sleep is free from limitations and rules. In a recent experiment participants were sleeping at their homes when their brain waves and other polysomnographic data were tracked remotely by a specially developed apparatus. When the server detected that the first participant entered a lucid dream, it generated a random Remmyo word and sent it to him via earbuds. The participant repeated the word in his dream, with his response captured and stored on the server. The next participant entered a lucid dream eight minutes later and received the stored message from the first participant. He confirmed it after awakening, marking the first-ever 'chat' exchanged in dreams.'

'Interesting,' thought Roman as he now pulled up and parked his surface-vehicle outside the mansion. He had arrived. Walking up to the door he halted and pressed the buzzer. Within a matter of seconds the door opened. It was Alexanko. He was a tall man with grey hair, and deep blue eyes, well dressed.

"Greetings Sir... You must be Roman Nebraska?"

"Correct..."

"I'm Alexanko. Please follow me."

He was led to the main living room. Alexanko opened the door with a smile and left. As Roman entered the room he saw John sitting on a large wooden chair dressed in a white garment. Roman was overwhelmed to finally see the Man from Proxima in the flesh. There was something otherworldly about him, the look in his green eyes. He had an unusual aura about him, a powerful presence. His face was slightly pale and gaunt, his light-brown hair slowly being invaded by grey. He was only fifty-eight, but he looked a lot older. Roman gazed around. Beautiful paintings covered the white coloured walls. One in particular stood out to him with a printed quote. It was a picture of the Milky Way and the quote read, 'Concerning matter, we have been all wrong. What we have called matter is energy, whose vibration has been so lowered as to be perceptible to the senses. There is no matter.'

"Please take a seat," invited John.

"Thank you, Sir," replied Roman. He sat down facing the Man from Proxima and it began...

"It is an honour to be here. I hope that you are feeling okay and are recovering well," said Roman pulling out his small notepad and pen from his jacket. He liked to interview people the old-fashioned way; after all it was the old-fashioned way, that is, a hand written letter that had secured him the very first interview with this amazing man. Shackleton was not looking entirely comfortable. In fact he had turned his piercing gaze Roman's way as if trying to read his soul. 'He's worried I'm going to sensationalise the story,' thought Roman. So to ease his man into the interview he started with something factual...

"Your historic voyage beyond the solar system is one that is revered by all. It was a journey that should have taken one-hundred-years but only took four due to the wormhole, remarkable in itself. This was humanity's first voyage beyond the solar system, heading to Alpha Centauri, the triple star system located in a different region of our galaxy, a leap into the unknown... Your name has been etched into history, Captain John Shackleton. Reaching the planet Proxima Centauri b which is 4.24 light years away... well, it didn't seem possible, but you, along with your crew made it there against all the odds, and as we speak the planet Proxima Centauri b is being terraformed. So firstly let me ask, how was the journey?"

"Well, let's just say it's an experience like no other. Travelling through the vastness of space leaves one feeling slightly insignificant." He paused clearing his throat and fell into a reverie for a moment. Roman did not disturb him. His mind was far in the past. "So, in terms of the actual journey itself I'll give you a quick breakdown. Including me and the other crew members, we were fifty in total. As for the spacecraft itself, it was piloted, completely controlled by machines, AI, high tech supercomputers. Incidentally the spacecraft was named Humanitas - Alpha Centauri. The spacecraft had originally launched from high-earth orbit firing up its nuclear fusion drive. It took fifteen days to accelerate under 1 g. to reach the cruising speed of 4.24 percent the speed of light. Using its nuclear fusion engine it took under two hours to pass the Moon and 14 days to pass the orbit of Mars. It was heading downwards 2.10 degrees below the ecliptic plane of the solar system. Of course the path was plotted to avoid any asteroids. The front of the spacecraft was built with reinforced layers to prevent erosion caused by interstellar dust and gas clouds."

Roman nodded but did not interrupt as he briskly made notes.

"It was a journey that would have taken one-hundred-years travelling at a rate of 4.24 percent the speed of light. In short, due to the wormhole, the long one-hundred-year journey was dramatically cut down to only four years. As we reached a certain point in space we entered the wormhole, the shortcut through space and time. It allowed the nuclear fusion spacecraft which was travelling at a rate of 4.24 percent the speed of light to travel from one point of the universe to another in almost a flash. In fact, had it not been for the wormhole the whole mission would have been vastly different and far more complex due to the one-hundred-year trip."

As he spoke, Shackleton seemed to lose some of the intenseness that had gripped him at the beginning as Roman had hoped. He decided to ask a few more questions about the journey before his questions became of a more personal nature.

"That's amazing and leads me on to two further questions about your journey. So, firstly, the wormhole that you traversed... Was it located prior to the journey?"

"Of course, that goes without saying. The spacecraft's inbuilt AI system –Omega, knows where all the traversable wormholes are according to the spacecraft's location. It can create a spatial map if you like. It was successfully used both ways, the journey there and when I was brought back to earth."

"Incredible..."

"At this point I think it will be beneficial to you, from an intellectual perspective, if I explain a little bit about wormhole detection. The best method to detect a wormhole is through the detection of radiation. The concept of the wormhole started in the early 20th century when Einstein proved the existence of an Einstein-Rosen bridge. Wormholes can, in fact, exist within the laws of thermodynamics. In short, if you were to combine exotic matter with a black hole, you would create a wormhole. However, if you were to attempt to make a wormhole with normal matter, it would be thermodynamically unstable and would collapse into the black hole. With reference to the field of physics, there are two main types of wormholes, the Lorentzian wormhole, which is a hole through space and time, and the Euclidian wormhole, which relies on particle physics and quantum mechanics. Lorentzian wormholes are interesting because of their special properties. First, they are stable and traversable both ways. These two unique properties allow for time travel, covering vast distances in an instant and then coming back. Another property special to wormholes is they do not have an event horizon, like their counterpart, the black hole. The lack of an event horizon, which is the boundary of a black hole through which no light or radiation can escape, is what allows the Lorentzian wormhole to be traversable.

Finally, to look for Lorentzian wormholes, we scientists can rely on properties thought to be specific to wormholes. The first is negative temperature, which arises from the distribution of exotic matter within the wormhole itself. With exotic matter thought to produce a negative temperature, the possibility exists that this property can be observed and measured as it has been. The second method is through the detection of certain types of radiation, but I think I'll stop there..."

Roman was deeply intrigued by what he was hearing although most of it was alien to him but for the sake of the flow of the interview he said, "Okay, now for the second question... You said that had it not been for the wormhole the whole mission would have been vastly different and far more complex due to the one-hundred-year trip. How so...?"

"Well firstly it would have required around 1,700 people to have bordered the flight. One-hundred-years is a long time. The initial crew members who were in command of the ship would eventually all perish. The initial crew members would never see Proxima Centauri b. Thus the children born during the flight would eventually take control of the ship. It would all be about the preservation of life, a new generation of humans taking command of the ship to ensure that they safely reached the planet. Of course there would have been strict reproduction guidelines. There would have been rules regarding family size to ensure each family had the same genetic influence on future generations and to avoid reducing genetic diversity. Each set of parents would have had to have a similar number of offspring... minimum of two and a maximum of three babies..."

Roman wrote down the information briskly. "I see. Please continue."

"Well, this would have been needed to maintain the replacement rate of the parents and at the same time avoid high population growth that would have strained onboard resources. Another important thing to mention here is that parents would have had to reproduce at different intervals to prevent age clusters of children. All these rules would have been put in place to avoid the collapse of the passenger population. I think I'll leave it there..."

"Sure," replied Roman. "Tell me something... Was the spacecraft that you travelled on big enough to have hypothetically accommodated 1,700 people if needed?"

"Yes, absolutely... For the fifty of us that went it was like living in a huge semi-empty city."

"Incredible. I just can't imagine it. Okay, tell me about your time on the planet and your cave experience of course."

Shackleton did not reply immediately and seemed to be choosing his words carefully.

"Well once we landed on the alien planet Proxima Centauri b, we soon established our base with domed habitats and research stations. As I'm sure you know Proxima Centauri b doesn't have a day/night cycle like Earth because it's tidally locked. This means that one side of the planet is always in daylight, while the other side is always in darkness. Naturally we landed and set up base on the side of that planet that experiences perpetual daylight. Anyhow, over time we began to explore the alien planet. Eventually we discovered vast underground caves. Then I had the encounter which has changed my life forever." Shackleton hesitated...

"Please, continue," encouraged Roman gently, deeply intrigued.

"Well, it happened like this... I went exploring on my own. As I entered a cave I saw a brilliant ball of fiery light." He paused for a second reflecting. "It hovered, pulsed and glowed. I started to inch closer to it, but before I knew it, a blinding beam of light projected out hitting my facemask and penetrating through. I dropped to the ground and at that very moment fell into a coma and remained like that for many, many years as you know. In terms of my return to earth, it was the American government and the Space Federation that decided that it was best, despite the long, complicated journey back. Two of the crew members flew back with me. I needed urgent assistance throughout. I had to be fed intravenously. Thus, out of the fifty people that landed on the alien planet Proxima b, only forty-seven remained there. What was strange was that although I was in a coma, that is, unable to speak or communicate at any level my eyes remained wide open throughout the ordeal."

"Yes," urged Roman. "I, as well as many others are aware of that. But what was that like? Were you able to process what you saw?"

"Okay..." John rubbed his gaunt face and continued... "Well, unbeknownst to the doctors at the time, and everyone else, the truth of the matter was that I was completely aware of my surroundings. I could see and hear absolutely everything. Eyes wide open and totally aware but not responsive at all. Eventually I broke free from whatever you want to call it, coma, etc... and returned to the world of the living."

There was a pause. Roman stopped scribbling and looked at his subject, intrigued. He noticed Shackleton was staring at him intently again and he felt an uncomfortable prickling on the back of his neck.

"Wow... this is fresh news to me." He exclaimed in an effort to move the interview on.

"It would be. The doctors decided to not share this information with the media. At least not for now... I'm not sure why exactly. Eventually it will leak out as it always does. Perhaps the doctors didn't want to be over bombarded by the media. However in time the world will know."

"This is totally bizarre. What did the doctors say when you told them all this?"

"They were all left stunned, ultimately unable to give answers. Maybe that's another reason why they haven't told the media yet. The whole notion that I was in a coma is now being reviewed."

"Well it doesn't sound like a coma to me. Anyway, it must have been very frustrating for you to be in such a state for all those years. Gosh... four years on a spacecraft returning to Earth and then another four in a hospital... A total of eight years..."

"Actually, the truth is it wasn't frustrating at all. Although I was completely aware of my surroundings and could see and hear absolutely everything it was as if I was frozen in time... as if time itself stood still. It's hard to explain. Anyway, the light told me that this was only going to be temporary and that my time would come. Time to enlighten the world... I was chosen to reveal a horrible truth."

Roman stared deeply into John's eyes, trying to gauge whether he was joking around but the expression on John's face was hard and serious as if he was about the reveal the ultimate truth.

"I'm sorry John but what are you talking about?"

"That brilliant ball of fiery light... That light spoke to me clearly and revealed something that has changed my life, as it will now change yours, forever. What that ball of light was exactly, remains a mystery, but it opened my eyes, and I agreed to this interview in order to open yours..."

"I don't understand. You're talking in riddles now. What do you mean exactly?"

"Roman what I'm about to share with you is something that will turn your world upside down. I am the only man alive, as far as I know, who is aware of the awful truth about our world. This truth was revealed to me by the light, and it has given me the power to open your eyes so that you can see for the very first time.

After reading your letter I did some research on you. I read all about your work as a paranormal investigator, explorer and freelance journalist. You have an enquiring and open mind. You are prepared to consider what most view as impossible. You tick all the boxes. I knew that you were the man that I needed to tell. It has to be the right person... someone who is psychologically strong, someone who is used to the bizarre. You are that person. I am not interested in interviews and money. My only interest is to recruit the right man; the man who can help me free the world from this evil."

Roman rubbed his jaw. In his work, he had heard all kinds of fantastic, mysterious stories, some beyond the bizarre. However, for a moment he wondered whether John was mentally unstable. 'Perhaps he's suffering from some kind of paranoia, a mental illness due to brain damage,' he thought to himself. But he suppressed this notion and remained completely professional.

He said in a calm voice, "Well I appreciate your faith in me, but I need to know, what exactly did the light tell you?"

In a perfectly normal voice with no hint of hysteria, Shackleton replied, "The light told me that our world is totally controlled by alien, reptilian creatures. These aliens came from the very planet we are terraforming, Proxima Centauri b. They have been here for hundreds of years. They all left Proxima b and targeted earth as their new home. They are the rulers of earth, the Puppet Masters."

Roman struggled to control his features. He was now convinced that John was mentally unstable, however this was the sort of thing he had engaged with for years working as a paranormal investigator and although it was unbelievable it excited him. He wanted to know more.

"Aliens...? Well I must admit I haven't seen any myself..."

"You can't. No one could, but now I can. You see the light not only spoke to me, but it opened my eyes so that I can now see the world as it really is. And it told me that I would have the power to make others see. By simply placing my hand on their forehead and filling them with a unique form of energy I can break them free from this mass hypnosis. These aliens disguise themselves as humans and use subliminal messages to control the masses. It's like the world is asleep. You need to be awakened. Then you will see them as they really are... the non-human faces... reptilian creatures under human flesh."

Composing himself, Roman said politely, "I'm sorry, but with all due respect this is simply unbelievable..."

"Roman I know it is, but it is the truth, as you will soon discover. When the light initially spoke to me, I too wondered whether I was suffering from some kind of delusion due to brain damage. But I've seen them myself, at the hospital, on the streets, on TV. They are everywhere."

Shackleton stood up, his face gaunt and pale. He stepped towards Roman who was still seated. Looking deeply into his eyes, he said, "Fear not. You will now be set free from this hypnosis and see for the first time."

Although Roman thought John was mentally unstable, he went along with it. He did not want to offend. He knew that John was a brilliant mind, a scientist, a legend but he had clearly lost his mind, even though he spoke with great clarity and confidence.

"Okay, I'm ready," Roman said with a faint voice, remaining professional throughout.

Shackleton placed his right hand on Roman's forehead and closed his eyes. It was as if he had disconnected his conscious mind from his bodily functions and become pure mind. Roman in turn didn't move. Closing his eyes he was surprised to feel a sudden surge of energy entering his body. He shook slightly and felt a warm tingle move through his chest. 'How weird,' he thought but dismissed it all the same.

Opening his eyes, he saw Shackleton slowly step back, turn and sit back down. He pressed his hands together and said, "That's it Roman. I have now accomplished what I set out to do. You have been released from the mass hypnosis, the first person on the planet to be set free."

Roman sat there unsure what to say. He had to continue to remain professional and not offend. He decided to remain silent and listen. At this point he felt it was best.

"Now please listen to me carefully, Roman. The light told me that these aliens are harmless as long as they think that you are asleep. If they suspect or know that you are awake they will kill you. Don't give any outward sign... I need to prepare you before you leave here. Please, you need to watch this..."

Via audio command Shackleton suddenly instructed the TV to activate. It was a programme about American politics and world affairs. Roman had seen the programme many times before. He focused on the screen but saw nothing out of the ordinary, just the usual human faces that would routinely pop up. But that was short lived. Suddenly a famous American politician was being interviewed, Chip Tatum, but he wasn't human. Eyes popping, Roman stared at the screen even as he jumped to his feet. The alien was speaking with a weird animal-like croak. For a split-second Roman felt his grasp on awareness waver. The grey reptilian head dissolved into the face of a human, a man. He rubbed his eyes as he fully awoke to see the grey headed alien once again. It was dressed in an elegant black suit with a tie. He began to study its face... Its head was smallish, hairless. It had two large snake-like eyes, a tiny nose, large mouth, and long ears. It looked hideous.

"I can't believe what I'm seeing," said Roman.

This was the ultimate paranormal experience. As the show proceeded, other aliens appeared across the screen with the odd human face here and there. All the aliens, both male and female looked exactly the same. Shackleton, via the remote, changed the channel. More aliens appeared across the screen. He changed it again. It was now the news channel. The two female news reporters were both aliens. Roman had seen enough.

"Okay, okay..." he said gesturing vaguely with trembling hands. This was the ultimate revelation. He couldn't quite believe what he had just seen. Shackleton was right. He sat back down, his face drained of colour, head down. He suddenly wondered whether Susan was really Susan, and whether Martin was really Martin. At this point nothing could be dismissed.

Deactivating the TV via audio command, Shackleton said with a clam, still voice, "Roman, I know that this is disturbing but you need to compose yourself. Do what is expected of you without any cracks. And when you see them, act normal. No eye-contact. These Puppet Masters are highly intelligent and will kill you if they know you are awake."

Raising his head up slowly, Roman asked, "Why are they here? And what do they want from us?"

"The Puppet Masters are no different from the Nazis, or the Huns from way back. Since the dawn of time there have always been groups that want to lead mankind. The only difference is that these things come from another planet, Proxima Centauri b. In short, these aliens view us as an inferior species and want to control us."

"Can these things reproduce?"

"Yes, but only amongst themselves, alien with alien. In short, there is no chance of some human-alien hybrid being produced. It can't happen. That's for sure."

"But I don't understand. How are they keeping everyone in this dream-like state?"

"The light told me that they send out signals. These signals alter brainwave activity, neuronal activity, cognitive function, altering reality. Human beings are living in an artificially induced state of consciousness. These aliens rule over Mankind because of the annihilation of consciousness. People are in a trance and have become slaves to the Puppet Masters."

"Signals, you say...?"

"Yes. These signals are what keep the human race in this trance-like state. Once these signals are intercepted, all the citizens of earth will see the Puppet Masters as they really are."

"Where are these signals coming from?"

"Machines... In short, one machine has been placed in every country across the planet in order to keep the citizens of earth under this mass hypnosis. Thus these signals are constantly being spread out across our world.

But the important thing to note here is if you deactivate one, all the others will in turn shut down. This is what the light told me. These machines operate symbiotically... Destabilize one you destabilize all, shutting them all down across the globe, nullifying all the signals respectively. Thus the seemingly all-knowing light only had to give me the location of one... the one here in the United States. My home country... And it did..."

"Okay, great, but where in the United States? The US is a big place. Where exactly is it located, or should I say, hidden?"

"Literally just under our noses..."

"You mean here in New York?"

"Yes. It has been hidden inside the Statue of Liberty would you believe.... Liberty, being the operative word... These aliens certainly have a sense of humour. As you know yourself Roman, back in the day people would go to Liberty Island; it was a great tourist attraction. They would visit the museum and get up close to the Statue. They would also go inside the Statue of Liberty and view it from inside. There were actual tours. Tourists would walk up the stairway or use the elevator which eventually led to the very top of the Statue. Upon reaching the top, its head, people would look out of the windows there. There was and probably still is a stairway that led to the torch for maintenance reasons. Anyhow, hypothetically speaking if we did miraculously find a way to get to Liberty Island safely avoiding detection and get inside the Statue of Liberty we would need to go all the way to the top. The machine is located by the head. That's where it operates."

"So that's why you can't get anywhere near the damn thing these days," snapped Roman angrily. "It's strictly forbidden and has been for just over a century now, ever since their arrival, I guess! The law states that the Statue of Liberty can only be viewed from afar. I've often wondered why Liberty Island and its old Liberty Museum were off limits to the public. Now it all makes sense."

"Yes! Liberty Island is constantly patrolled by the military... them... the Puppet Masters! We simply can't attempt to take a boat across or even swim it. Soldiers are on guard on a 24-hour basis. Not to mention that police-hover-jets periodically fly inspection flights around Liberty Island. Then you have the surveillance cameras. The only boats that are allowed to go to Liberty Island are police and military boats... the Puppet Masters."

"So what do we do?"

"In short the Statue of Liberty must be destroyed somehow from afar. If we destroy the Statue of Liberty, blowing off its head, we destroy the machine inside, deactivating it. As a result all the other machines across the planet will shut down, halting all signals. Mankind will then awaken, and the war will start..."

"Yes, I guess we will have to find a way of blowing it up from afar..."

"Correct."

"But how...?"

"With some type of weapon... The only problem is it won't be easy to get hold of such a weapon. But we must find a way to get hold of one somehow. Once we do we can then plan to blow the Statue of Liberty up targeting the head from afar. That's the best and safest way to deactivate the machine. Don't worry we will find a way. Humanity needs to awaken soon." He paused for a moment then said, "The Statue of Liberty stands 305 feet tall. All it is... is a load of copper castings attached to the steel framework. Steel is a non-combustible material and consequently does not burn. Steel does not melt at temperatures typically encountered in a building fire... but the Statue's copper shell, its skin, can be easily destroyed along with the machine which is located inside by the head."

Roman listened quietly. The look in Shackleton's eyes showed that he considered the matter settled. Rubbing his head Roman got to his feet. He was caught in a daze, his mind still battling with the horrifying reality that now faced him. The world he thought he knew was now no more.

"Roman," said Shackleton sharply. "Remember what I told you. You must remain composed at all times. Now that your eyes have been opened, go back home and get some rest if you can. We will meet here again very soon. Here, take this card. My private number is on it."

Roman took the card and placed it into his jacket pocket. He then asked, "What about recruiting? Telling others about what's happening...?"

"It's far too dangerous. You just can't know how a person will react to such a revelation. You have many unique qualities that make you suited but even so I took a risk. I haven't even told my long-time friend, Alexanko. We can't afford any slip ups. Besides, there's no need. I only need one, you. You and I alone can deactivate the machine, and free the human race globally," he said emphatically.

Roman drove his surface-vehicle home, the sun shimmering above him in the atmosphere. The ozone layer was almost gone. Ultraviolet and gamma rays were battering the surface of the Earth. The high-energy particles were knocking atmospheric molecules apart, oxygen, nitrogen, to produce nitrogen dioxide. Inside his surface-vehicle, Roman focused on the road ahead. He'd had plenty time to think and digest the horrible truth about the state of the world. He made himself thoroughly familiar with what needed to be done after Shackleton's revelation. Destroy the Statue of Liberty by targeting its head from afar and in turn destroy the machine, deactivating it. It seemed so simple but how would they do it...? A powerful weapon would be needed and where would they get that from? He saw a park. It was neat and clean; the lawns glittered and insects hummed, seeking moisture from the stalks of sweet-smelling flowers. Children scampered and shouted. 'If only these children really knew what was happening to their world,' he thought bitterly.

Ahead the city loomed, its stern columns of office buildings sharply outlined against the sky. As he entered the city he began to see the non-human faces here and there; heart-stopping moments. The streets swarmed with noise and activity. And the aliens seemed to be omnipresent. He abruptly decided to pull over and park. He stepped out of the surface-vehicle and began to walk, reminding himself that he needed to blend in with the crowds and act normal, as normal as possible. He pushed on, carefully avoiding any indication that he saw the

Puppet Masters. In the store windows he could see vid-phones for sale alongside mixers and toasters. At intervals along the street, Roman would stop, pretending that he was looking for something, but in actuality, he was carefully studying the relationship between human and beast as they poured in and out of bars, some walking across the streets arrogantly amongst the hypnotised humans. Some of the aliens drove by in surface-vehicles. Others entered restaurants, some standing and chatting to people, humans. 'Termites...! These things are like termites... social insects. Individually they appear to be almost helpless and dumb,' he thought to himself. But appearances were deceiving. Individually they were far more intelligent than man, and as a colony they were like an unapproachable roaring beast.

He entered a bar. It was mainly filled with humans... men in rumpled business suits, trying to read their newspapers and drink beer. But he could see the odd alien face here and there, their small hairless heads, and large sinister snake-like eyes. 'How ugly can you be?' he thought in disgust. He noticed one standing at the bar with its tiny nose, large mouth, and long ears reading a paper. Most of the time the voices that echoed around in the bar were human, but now and then he heard the strange animal-like croaks. Composing himself he walked over to the bar and sat. He had to be careful. Standing around for too long analysing and not responding the way the others did might alert one of them. They might start to suspect that he was awake.

Double shot of whiskey, please," he said calmly to the neat looking brunette barmaid. He carefully looked at the alien once again, the one standing at the bar. Again, for a split-second, the reptilian alien faded a little, and

Roman saw the flickering image of a thin man. His mind spun. He rubbed his eyes. The flickering image of the thin man was no more. He was once again looking at an alien. Although awake, it seemed to him that from time to time he would almost be pulled back into that state of hypnosis, but it would only be for a split-second. Shackleton's healing hands had ultimately worked.

Knocking back the whiskey he glanced at the TV set which was fixed to the wall. One of the aliens was on, live. He could just about hear it. It was talking about what men needed to do to attract women. Printed across the screen was the following:

Dr. Harry Carpenter – expert consultant – how to attract women

At this point, Roman laughed. 'What a joke... expert consultant! How to attract women... Boy if only they could all see your ugly face,' he thought. The alien by the bar suddenly turned and looked at him. Had his laughter caused suspicion, he wondered. With a nod Roman smiled at him trying to remain calm. In turn the alien nodded back and said, "Expert consultant, eh! How ridiculous can you get? If you need a consultant to tell you how to attract a lady, you've got to have serious problems." It started to laugh, a rich hideous laughter that rang in Roman's ears and echoed in his mind. Suppressing his desire to smash its face in with his fist, Roman calmly replied, "That's for sure, buddy."

The alien continued to laugh. Roman could take no more. Frustration soon turned swiftly to sheer terror as the reality of the situation once again penetrated his consciousness. Paying the lady he left the bar and walked out onto the busy street blinking at the sea of faces. Three police officers stormed by with an air of authority. They were aliens but they had no power over him. None of them did. Only he and Shackleton could see the world as it really was.

Roman finally reached home glad to escape the chaos outside his walls. It was dark and the night was very still. The hours had flown by. He had passed through successive phases of despair, anger, fear; now he was calm again, although his mind, searching for ways of escape, was too active to allow sleep. With a deliberate and determined effort of will, he turned his thoughts once more toward the problem of rescue... rescue for the human race. It seemed so simple... Shackleton had told him how it needed to be accomplished... Destroy the Statue of Liberty targeting its head from a distance and in turn you destroy the machine that is hidden inside it, the machine that is sending out these signals and causing the mass hypnosis here in the United States. By deactivating the machine here you will in turn deactivate all the other machines across the globe. But how would they get the weapon needed for such a task? It would not be easy. Regardless, the aliens needed to be exposed and then the war with humanity would begin.

He started to think about all the non-human faces he had seen in the city. It made him boil. Turning on the TV via audio command, the first face he saw was an alien. Instantly he deactivated the TV set. He began to think about his friends, Susan, Martin, and all the others. "What if I discover that they are all aliens?" he muttered to himself in horror. "They can't be... Not Susan, not Martin, surely...?"

He was tempted to make a video call, one to Susan and then one to Martin but it was getting late. He began to think about the discussion he'd had with Martin... the discussion concerning Bigfoot, the great sea serpent, and some of the alien-like creatures beneath the ocean. Ironically the sea was probably a safer place than the land. Aliens from another world were actually here on planet Earth roaming the streets, the cities, controlling the world... literal aliens. This was the ultimate paranormal story he had to share with his friends, the world, and it was completely factual. If Martin proved to be human, and he would soon find out, telling him about the reality of the world concerning the reptilian creatures would blow his mind completely. Of course he would have to take him to Shackleton's first so that he too would see them in their real form, otherwise Martin would think he was insane, so too Susan.

How could anyone possibly believe such a thing after all? The problem was that Shackleton didn't want anyone else to know, not even his long-time friend and personal assistant Alexanko. But to Roman, numbers were important. The more people that knew, the better... If Martin and Susan proved to be human he felt it was his duty to help free them from the mass hypnosis immediately. But this would be something that he would have to discuss with Shackleton first. It was a very delicate situation. If Shackleton agreed he would take both Susan and Martin over to his home. From there they would be awakened.

He stood up and paced around the living room and started to think about the cryptic symbols and carvings that had been discovered on Proxima Centauri b. 'The aliens responsible for them were now here,' he thought in disgust. In anger he said out loud, "If only the people out there on Proxima Centauri b knew what was actually happening down here..." But there was no way to relay such a message to them; after all they were in another region of the galaxy. He tried to picture it... mankind on another planet far out, but it soon faded into an unreachable haze. Unable to sleep or rest, he impulsively decided that he needed to go for a drive.

He drove aimlessly. It was late. He checked the time. It was 10:33pm. The radio was on low volume, and the words of a famous philosopher, Norman Finkelstein, drifted towards him... 'Many and strange are the universes that drift like bubbles in the foam upon the River of Time.' He changed the radio station at random hoping to find some soft comforting music. But instead he found the science channel. A scientist was being interviewed, Alfred Cohen. He said, 'Quantum teleportation has one pivotal property: it is impossible to create an identical copy of a quantum state without destroying the original. In fact you must destroy the original arrangement in order to extract all the necessary information from it to construct the new teleported state.' Roman turned the radio off. He was in no mood for philosophy and science. His mind remained fixed on one thing alone.... the destruction of the aliens.

After a short while he pulled up and parked. He was on the outskirts of the city. For a split moment he felt alone in the cosmos. Along with Shackleton he was the only other person that knew what was happening. It suddenly filled him with a sense of awe and importance. Stepping out of the surface-vehicle he started to walk. The street was bare. The air was icy cold. Above he could see the Moon, that ancient enigma, as it orbited Earth in its elliptical plane. Overhead, a flight of birds passed. Hunched over he moved on. His interview with John Shackleton haunted him. He relived it in his mind and replayed it almost to the point that he had it memorized. Suddenly he heard a metallic sound. It was a black cat seeking food from an empty can. He watched it for a moment and moved on. In the distance he suddenly noticed a female alien walking towards him. It was dressed as if it had been to a party, short skirt, high heels. He kept calm watching it with revulsion. As it walked by him it suddenly stopped. Hanging around its neck was a silver necklace glittering with coloured stones.

"Hey handsome... Where are you going?" it squawked.

Roman felt sick. Not only had the aliens invaded his world, but they also wanted to be intimate with the citizens of earth. And it was happening on a daily basis. Thankfully it wouldn't lead to anything... Aliens could only breed with their own kind. He suddenly wondered whether his ex-girlfriend Tessa was one of them. He felt disgusted at the thought. Unsure what to say he remained silent for a moment. The alien's snake-like eyes lit up and were menacing.

"Hey, what's wrong handsome?"

Yet again, for a split-second the image blurred. For a moment he could see a pretty blonde standing there. Then next, the hideous alien thing. He had to remain composed. It had to think that he was in a trance like the others. If it knew he was awake he would have to kill it somehow. But that would be a dangerous move. The city was filled with hidden surveillance cameras.

Calmly he replied, trying to mask his revulsion, "Look lady, I'm sorry, I've had a busy day."

He moved on walking away at pace. The alien in turn said nothing, walking away in the opposite direction. After circling the area for a good thirty minutes, deep in thought and trying to come to terms with the horrifying reality of the world, Roman saw a police vehicle approaching. As it got nearer he could see two non-human faces, the aliens. He was overwhelmed by fear but remained calm. He wondered what they wanted from him. Did they suspect that he was awake? The police vehicle pulled up near him. Roman's heart began to beat hard. The driver's side window lowered. He could now see a hideous grey face. Again he studied its features... its smallish grey hairless head, its two large snake-like eyes, tiny nose, large mouth, long ears.

"Late night walk, eh?" It said with a grin bordering on the sinister.

At once Roman tried to mask his resentment and for a brief second the veil that hid his inner thoughts, his hatred and disgust, seemed to tremble and liquefy. But then composing himself Roman replied, "Yes, needed some fresh air."

The alien was now staring hard at Roman as if ready to pounce, so too the other one who was sitting silently on the passenger seat. Roman, although gripped in fear, remained calm. It was vital.

"Do you have your ID with you?" It said with its usual animal-like voice.

From his jacket, the upper pocket, Roman pulled out his ID card. He gave it to the alien cop. It looked at the card and then returned it to Roman.

"Okay, Mr Nebraska, have a good night,"

The police vehicle pulled away and slowly drove off disappearing into the distance. The danger was over yet it was a nerve-racking experience. After some reflection, he decided that it was best to return to his surface-vehicle and head home.

Roman was in bed asleep. In his dream he could see gardens bright with strange flowers. There were streams that trickled gently between moss-grown rocks. He could see mountains, oceans, a blue sky... The blue sky soon turned pitch black. He was now enveloped in total darkness. The face of an alien suddenly appeared in the darkness wreathed in mist. His face convulsed and he awoke, sweating profusely.

It was morning and the sun shone brightly in a cloudless sky. He rose from his bed and stretched. Walking into the kitchen he sat at the table and poured himself a glass of orange juice. The juice was warm but he gulped it down refreshing his pallet. Today was the big day. He would call both Susan and Martin; vid-phone call. If they proved to be human as he believed they were he would then call John Shackleton and tell him that he wanted to bring them round to his place, reassuring him that they could be trusted fully so that they too could be awakened.

Numbers were important as far as Roman was concerned. He would have to give it his best shot to convince John. He recalled John's words vividly during the interview... 'It's far too dangerous. You just can't know how a person will react to such a revelation. You have many unique qualities that make you suited but even so I took a risk. I haven't even told my long-time friend, Alexanko. We can't afford any slip ups. Besides, there's no need. I only need one, you. You and I alone can deactivate the machine, and free the human race globally...' He would have to try really hard to convince him, but Roman knew that telephone calls would be occasionally monitored by the authorities, or as he now knew the aliens, so he would have to be extra careful when calling him. He had to be discreet and yet relay the message and his intentions clearly. Perhaps speaking to John face to face would be safer and it would give him a better chance of convincing him. But he would still need to call him to fix the appointment.

Rushing over to the vid-phone, Roman halted, breathed in deeply and then dialled Susan's home number trying to compose himself. If she wasn't at home the call would be redirected to her cell phone. Within seconds Susan's human face appeared on the screen in ripples of visual static. The static cleared and the screen was now bright and sharp. He was so relieved. His heart thudded with delight.

"Hi Roman," she said smiling as always, "I was just about to step out of the house. I'm heading to the office. Got some work to catch up on... I'm writing a new article. Are you coming in today? I'm dying to know how the interview went with the Man from Proxima..."

Steadily Roman replied, "I might be coming in later. As for the interview... let's just say it was very enlightening."

"I bet it was. I can't wait to hear the full story."

'Full story indeed,' thought Roman.

"Okay, Roman. I've got to dash. Hopefully I will see you later. Bye for now..."

As the call deactivated he prepared himself for the next. Again he dialled. This time Martin's home number... He waited. Suddenly Martin's human face appeared on the screen. Again a great sense of relief passed over him.

"Good morning my friend," smiled Martin. How did the interview go?"

He steadied himself, clearing his throat and replied, "Let's just say it was one hell of an interview."

"I can imagine. Well you'll need to fill me in with all the details."

"I will... that's for sure..." Roman's mind was now focused on speaking with John.

"Perhaps we can meet up later?"

"I'll let you know Martin..."

Martin suddenly sensed that something wasn't quite right with Roman. That fact had bypassed Susan but Martin had known him a long time. The pattern of Roman's behaviour had not changed yet Martin sensed something wasn't quite right.

"Roman, are you okay? You just seem a bit off. Maybe it's just me."

"I'm fine Martin. Just a little tired..."

"Are you sure?"

"Yes. Look I'll call you later."

"Okay my friend. I'm looking forward to hearing what the Man from Proxima had to say to you. Connect later."

Roman deactivated the call. He breathed in deeply. Both Susan and Martin were human. Now that it was confirmed it was time to call John. He rushed over to his jacket which was placed on the sofa and removed the card that John had given him. John's private number was on it. Moving back over to the vid-phone he promptly dialled but with the intention of organizing an appointment so that he could see him face to face. He decided that it was far too risky to speak over the phone, not to mention that he had a better chance of convincing John if he saw him in person. John's gaunt face formed across the screen.

"Roman..."

"Yes, John, it's me. Look I need to talk to you. It's important. When can I come over?"

Seconds of weighted silence passed...

"How about now...?"

John checked the time. It was 10:15am.

"That works. See you shortly..."

Guided by Alexanko, Roman entered the same room as before - the main living room. John was sitting in the same large wooden chair dressed in the same white garment. It was almost a repeat of the interview.

Taking a seat Roman got straight to the point... "John, I know that you don't want anybody else knowing about this alien invasion that is taking place under our very noses, but I'm sorry, I think you're wrong."

John remained composed. He looked deeply into Roman's eyes and replied, "Why?"

"There is strength in numbers. At least it helps psychologically if nothing else. Think about it. You chose to tell me, a complete stranger. We never met before. You selected me and only me to interview you with the intention of telling me about the alien invasion. You recruited me due to what you found on the net, my CV, etc, my past experiences and decided I was the one... You knew that having an extra person would be much more beneficial to you in your attempt to deactivate the machine and expose these beasts. Attempting to do it alone would have been much harder. You trusted in me and now the job has already been cut in half. So... please trust in me again regarding this... I have two friends Susan and Martin. They are good friends, and they are people you can trust, both intelligent and courageous. I would like to bring them to you here at the mansion so that you can explain to them what is happening, followed by the awakening. I want them to see and be free from the mass hypnosis."

John rubbed his jaw thoughtfully. His initial instruction was now being challenged. During his career, he had always given the orders and others just quietly followed.

In the cut and thrust of his life as a man of science, the captain of a spacecraft, a space pioneer, he had given quarter to none. He surprised himself when he replied, "I do see your logic. Maybe I have been too cautious. I guess you are right. I trusted in you, a complete stranger at the time. I guess if we recruit two more people that you recommend it won't be an overload."

At once Roman felt a great sense of relief. He had achieved his objective. He felt his cheeks flush. He had expected a potential quarrel. "Great, there are many advantages when you recruit the right people. The power of many minds unified..."

John sat back on his large wooden chair, and said, "Roman I'm a hard man, but open to logical suggestion. And your suggestion makes sense taking into consideration all the factors. Anyhow ultimately it's all about deactivating the machine that's hidden inside the Statue of Liberty. And I've already told you how that needs to be done, the only way possible. The only problem that now remains is how do we get the weapon needed for such a task? It won't be easy, but we need to find a way. Once we've achieved that, we can accomplish the task... then it will be a new dawn for mankind. A turning point in history. It is true that no man can foresee the future, the endless consequences of his actions, but one thing I do know is that the world will be a much better place once we expose and destroy these alien things." He paused in thought for a second. "The mental evolution of this race of aliens does fascinate me, I must say." Anyhow, you can bring your friends here tonight and I will do the rest. Say, 9 o'clock."

Roman stood up and stepped towards John. He then knelt before him with due respect. A bond had formed. Complete trust...

"Thank you John. I'll organise everything. I will then call you to confirm..."

Back at home Roman had the TV on. The day was passing fast and when the presenter announced it was time for the five o'clock news he double checked with his watch. He had made the necessary calls to both Susan and Martin telling them that he had been invited over to John's mansion for a drink and if they wanted they could come with him. Roman went on to tell them that it would be a unique opportunity, a unique experience meeting the Man from Proxima. After all, he was a legend, the ultimate space pioneer, a living piece of history. How could they refuse? To give them that final push he told them that John was expecting them and that he had told John all about them. Both happily accepted. Roman had arranged to pick Susan up at 8pm and they would then go on to Martin's. Susan and Martin had never officially met. This was going to be the first time. The actual meeting with John had been fixed for 9pm. He had called John to confirm that he'd organized everything accordingly and that he would be there with his friends as planned.

Pacing nervously around the living room Roman walked over to the small bar. He grabbed a bottle of whiskey and a small glass and moved over to the sofa and sat. He poured a couple of fingers and placed the bottle on the table before him. He rubbed his eyes and knocked back the liquor. It was enough to relax him a little and calm his nerves. He knew that Susan's and Martin's lives were about to change drastically. 'It was for the better,' he thought. Then for a moment he wondered how they would react. Regardless they needed to know. The ultimate goal was to deactivate the machine. Grabbing the remote he raised the volume and flicked through the channels until he saw one of them. He looked at it, almost studying it in revulsion. By now he was used to them, as ugly as they were. It was dressed in dark brown shorts and a cream-coloured shirt with short sleeves. It had a rucksack on its back and was in a jungle.

It said, "The Amazon jungle is full of deadly creatures... animals that can kill you at any moment."

Roman laughed and then said, "What a joke." He was slightly tipsy. The whiskey had hit the spot. He could not resist the little jab.

Again the alien said, "What is the most cunning of all the animals? That which no man has yet seen..."

Roman in a fit of sudden anger stood up looking directly at the alien on the TV screen... "What is the most cunning of all the animals? That which no man has yet seen... Indeed, how ironic that you should be saying this, you ugly beast. The other helpless humans watching this can't see you as you truly are, but I can..." Rubbing his eyes he composed himself and sat back down. He changed the channel and saw another alien. He grimaced. They were literally everywhere. This time the alien was dressed in a light-blue suit, white shirt, green tie. It was being interviewed by young blond a lady, a human. At this point Roman felt like deactivating the TV. He felt sick. But due to a sudden morbid twisted curiosity he decided to hear the alien out.

The lady suddenly asked it with a soft innocent voice, "So Professor Peter Walsh, how many copies have you sold since you published your first book titled... Inside the Mind of Erwin Schrödinger?"

Its reply was filled with arrogance, "Well, I published my first book three weeks ago. And I have already sold 7,000 copies. I mainly focus on Schrödinger's wave equation. Schrödinger's wave equation is a partial differential equation that governs the wave function of a quantum mechanical system. The Schrödinger equation has two forms: the time dependent and the time independent."

"Just out of interest Professor Walsh why did you chose Schrödinger? There have been many great scientists..."

"No real reason. I just decided to focus on him in my first book. I will write others in due course. His equation changed the world. But there have been many others of course, like Pythagoras's Theorem, Euler's Formula for Polyhedra, Navier-Stokes Equation, Maxwell's Equations in Electrodynamics, Dirac's Equation in Quantum Field Theory, Heisenberg's Uncertainty Principle, and so forth... However, I think that my next book will be based on Einstein... Relativity! In simplistic terms the theory of Relativity can be quickly summed up in six sentences: Light speed remains constant. Time is the 4th dimension. Gravity is the curvature of space time. Gravity travels in the form of waves. The faster you move through space the slower you move through time. Time slows down around heavy objects."

"Fascinating, Professor... Tell me more..." simpered the interviewer.

"Well, Einstein shook the foundations of physics with his theories of relativity. He revealed that time itself is not separate but part of a four-dimensional continuum called space-time. Gravity, once thought of as a simple force, was redefined as the bending of this space-time fabric."

Roman switched the TV off. He'd heard enough. He shook his head in an angry gesture of defiance. He began to think... 'This damn alien has certainly done its homework and has now published a book that is selling well, fit for human scholastic consumption. These beasts are too clever, but their reign will come to an end...' He composed himself and leaned back to relax. He closed his eyes, not to sleep but to try and block out the feelings of calamity that threatened to engulf him. When he opened his eyes again and checked his watch it was 7:15pm. He leapt up. It was time to get ready.

Roman pressed the buzzer on the mansion door. It was dark outside, but the darkness was somewhat illuminated by the mansion's outside lights. They looked like they belonged in an old castle, silent flames of fiery yellow. A cold wind blew. The stars sparkled. The moon hung bright. Susan and Martin stood behind him admiring the white mansion. The door opened. It was Alexanko just as he expected, dressed in a grey suit, white shirt, no tie.

But this time Alexanko seemed different. He looked deeply into Roman's eyes and rubbed his shoulder warmly. There was a sparkle in his eyes, a sparkle that he had initially lacked. Roman was convinced that he was now 'awake' and that John had enlightened him, after all he was his personal assistant and good friend, not to mention that John had agreed to enlighten both Susan and Martin, so why not his friend too? It would soon be confirmed. As before, Alexanko led Roman into the living room but this time came in with him, Susan and Martin following behind. Roman now knew for certain that Alexanko was awake.

Susan blushed prettily and said, "It's an honour to be here, Sir. Thank you for inviting me. You have a beautiful home. It's a lovely mansion. Had you remained up there on Proxima b, this mansion would have gone to waste." She blushed even deeper when she realised she was tongue-tied and babbling. Roman had to hold in an affectionate chuckle.

"Firstly it's a pleasure to meet you." John replied smoothly. "And thank you for the complement. As for the mansion going to waste, well my friend Alexanko lives here too. He always has, ever since I purchased it five years before my historic journey. Back then I had no idea that I would be leaving the planet potentially forever."

"I see," Susan answered, her voice warming with pleasure.

Martin spoke, next, seemingly calm and suave on the outside but Roman could sense the excitement that lay beneath, "Greetings Sir. I'm delighted to be here."

"My pleasure... Please, help yourself to a drink and take a seat."

On the table was a bottle of red wine, a bottle of whiskey, a carton of orange juice, two cans of coke and two cans of beer. There were also five empty glasses. Susan and Martin advanced, both curious and slightly hesitant. They sat beside each other on the sofa; the newcomers. Neither chose to pour a drink. As for Roman he picked up a can of beer and sat. Alexanko took his seat reaching for a coke. Finally John sat down on his large wooden chair, this time dressed in a grey garment that fell whispering to the floor. He rubbed his hands.

Susan smiling suddenly asked," So what's it like up there? Space I mean?"

"There is a timelessness about space flight... it's a unique experience."

She then asked, "Have you always had an interest in science, since you were a kid, I mean?"

"Yes, I've always loved science for as long as I can remember. And I've always had a deep desire to know more about our universe. This led me to become the man I am today. I'm one of many. There have been many great minds throughout the course of time. For centuries, humanity has looked up at the stars and asked questions that echo through time: What is the universe? Are we alone? These questions form the foundation of curiosity driving us to explore, discover and imagine. From the minds of ancient philosophers to modern scientists like me, the pursuit of knowledge has revealed a universe far stranger and more beautiful than we could have ever imagined. From the dawn of time, men like me have sought answers to the greatest mysteries pertaining to our universe. Ancient stargazers looked up into the night sky and charted the heavens, believing the stars held the keys to understanding the universe. Philosophers pondered the structure of reality. Questions that have echoed throughout time... What lies beyond the veil of perception? Is our universe part of a much larger hidden tapestry, one woven with dimensions beyond our wildest imagination? The idea that we live in a three-dimensional universe plus time is an illusion of our limited perception... We see a three-dimensional world around us and accept its constraints as absolute, but there are other dimensions invisible to our senses."

Roman smirked. 'Invisible to our senses, yes, indeed,' he thought. He liked the way John was handling the delicate situation. He was slowly, intellectually paving his way to telling them about the reality of the world... the alien invasion. His brilliant mind was magnetic, captivating. Susan and Martin were in awe of him. Roman could see it. John continued...

"However, with the right tools, mathematics, physics, and imagination, we can begin to unveil the hidden dimensions that shape the universe. In order to imagine higher dimensions, we must step outside our conventional way of thinking. Think of a shadow. A shadow is a two-dimensional projection of a three-dimensional object. It lacks depth and detail, yet it hints at the true form of the object casting it. In a similar way, our universe might be a shadow of a higher dimensional reality. What we perceive as separate forces... gravity, electromagnetism, and the nuclear forces may actually be unified when viewed from a higher dimensional perspective..."

"This is fascinating stuff, very deep," enthused Martin. "Other dimensions invisible to our senses... Mind-blowing...!"

John suddenly stood up staring at both Martin and Susan. His expression changed. He looked serious.

"Yes Martin, there are many things invisible to our senses. But there is one thing in particular that you need to know about, and I have the power for you and Susan to awaken and see the world as it really is at present."

Martin turned to look at Susan. She eyed him sharply. Both were slightly perturbed and confused. They looked over at Roman wondering whether John was joking. It sounded too bizarre.

Roman felt the need to say something to them; something to calm them, reassure them. He almost felt guilty, but they needed to know the truth. Addressing both of them, he said in a calm caring voice, "Please listen to what John has to say, it's vitally important. Trust me…"

Without replying they silently turned their heads focusing on John as he stood there with authority. He had a powerful presence.

Susan, who was now boiling with curiosity, suddenly asked, "What's this all about exactly, John?"

"Please indulge me," replied John, softly. "I'm going to reveal something to both of you that will change your lives forever. Your friend Roman already knows… so does Alexanko."

Roman nodded at Alexanko and smiled.

Rubbing his head John continued, "Let me start by saying this. My cave experience was the most enlightening experience that I have ever had. Yes, it put me into what many believed was a coma for many, many years. I guess it had to be that way. But ironically it opened my eyes... In short, I saw a brilliant ball of fiery light inside that cave. It hovered, pulsed and glowed. And before I knew it, a blinding beam of light projected out hitting my facemask and penetrating through..." He paused for a moment in reflection and then began to recount the incident in the cave with the mysterious light that he had told Roman about in the interview with all the other details...

Silence fell on all of them as he finished his tale. He poured himself an orange juice, took a sip and then continued, "Years of my life passed by, and I was unable to communicate with the living. But I held it together because I knew my time would come. A time to enlighten the world... I was chosen to reveal the truth. Don't get me wrong I had my moments of intense frustration, especially knowing what I know, not to mention the fact that I could see them during my time at the hospital. Some of them were nurses, doctors, visitors. Of course I wasn't shocked by this because the light had opened my eyes and revealed all to me up in that cave."

Scratching his forehead, Martin suddenly asked, "See them? Who's them?"

"I will answer that in due course. Now back to the light... That light spoke to me clearly and revealed everything to me. What that ball of light actually was remains a mystery but it opened my eyes and you are here tonight so I can open yours. Everything was revealed to me by that light and I now have the power to open your eyes so that you can see for the very first time."

Summoning a little courage, red-cheeked, Susan asked tamely, "Please, you are not making sense. What are you trying to say?"

"The point is this Susan. Our world is totally controlled by aliens, reptilian creatures."

Susan's jaw dropped. Martin's face drained of colour.

When he found his voice Martin said, "What the hell? What are you talking about?"

"Our world is totally controlled by aliens, reptilian creatures. These aliens came from Proxima Centauri b, they very planet that I and my crew journeyed to... the very planet that is being terraformed by humans as we speak. Had it not been for my cave encounter I would have still been there."

"This is something else," snapped Martin, glaring at Roman.

Roman promptly interjected with a calm, steady voice, "Martin, listen to him. It's all true. Believe me. I was the one who convinced him to tell you and Susan about this awful truth so that you could be awakened. I organised this meeting. Originally he didn't want to tell anyone, including Alexanko, but me. He only wanted me to know, but I convinced him others needed to know also. Please, listen to him..."

Silently Martin shrugged and then turned his head to look at John. "Okay, tell me more..."

"These aliens have been here for hundreds and hundreds of years. They all left Proxima b and targeted earth as their new home. In short, they are the rulers of earth, the Puppet Masters."

ANTONY FUCILLA

"Aliens, you say. Well I must admit I haven't seen any myself," snapped Martin, impatient with the line of conversation.

"Nor me," whispered Susan, her disappointment in the progress of the meeting palpable on her face.

"Let me explain something to you. The reason you haven't seen these aliens is because you can't. No one can, unless awakened via my power, the power that the light gave me. Roman and Alexanko were both blind, but now they can see and are fully awake. The light in that cave not only spoke to me but it opened my eyes so that I can see the world as it really is, and it told me that I would have the power to make others see by simply placing my hand on their forehead and filling them with an energy that would break them free from this mass hypnosis."

"Are you saying that Susan and I are both hypnotised?" demanded Martin indignantly.

"Yes... The only people on the planet, who can see, who are awakened are me, Roman and Alexanko. These aliens disguise themselves as humans and use subliminal messages to control the masses. It's like the world is asleep, in a trance."

"It's all true," said Alexanko suddenly. "This morning I woke up as usual, thinking I knew the world around me. But then John spoke to me and explained everything just like he is now. Like you Martin, Susan, I was left dumbfounded. It is hard to believe I know. But after I was awakened and could see, I knew it was all true. From 6pm today, I have seen the world as it really is. You need to be awakened. Then you will see them as they really are... the non-human faces... reptilian creatures under human flesh."

John smoothly interjected, "Up in that cave on Proxima Centauri b, when the light initially told me, I wondered whether I was suffering from some kind of delusion due to brain damage. But of course that is far from the truth. I've seen them everywhere, at the hospital, on the streets, on TV. Anyway it's time for you both to awaken. Please remain seated." John stood up smiling at them to reassure them that they had nothing to worry about. He stepped over towards them as they sat silently on the sofa. Neither moved away but Susan glanced at Roman for reassurance. He felt a wave of relief as it appeared they had accepted the awful truth and were prepared to go along with the proceedings.

"Don't be afraid," murmured John, "You will be set free from this hypnosis and see for the first time." He closed his eyes and gently placed his right hand on Martin's forehead and his left on Susan's. They both shook slightly and Roman knew they were feeling that strange energy entering their bodies and feeling a warm tingle move through their chests. Opening his eyes, John slowly stepped back, turned and returned to his seat. He said, "Okay, you have been set free from this mass hypnosis."

Both Susan and Martin looked at each other and then around the room at the others.

"That's it?" asked Susan sharply.

"Yes... that's it. But now, listen to me very carefully. The light told me that these aliens are harmless as long as they think that you are asleep. If they suspect or know that you are awake they will kill you."

Martin shuddered at the thought. He then said, "Okay, why don't you put on the TV. Let's see these aliens."

"That's exactly what I had in mind. You need to be prepared before you leave here. The best and only way is to use the TV so that you can see them and know that what I've told you is completely true. These aliens take some getting used to..."

Via audio command, John instructed the TV to activate. All eyes in the room focused on the screen. Different people, humans, appeared... It was a film, a movie, with only humans visible. John changed the channel. This time there were adverts playing. Again, only human faces could be seen but then suddenly they all saw an alien. Then another popped up. Both Susan's and Martin's eyes grew wide in horror. John changed the channel again. It was the news channel. A female alien news reporter, elegantly dressed, was now visible, sitting there speaking with an animal-like croak. For a split-second both Susan and Martin felt their grasp on awareness waver. The reptilian grey head dissolved into the face of a woman. They rubbed their eyes as they fully awoke to see the grey headed female alien once again. In revulsion they both studied its face... its hairless smallish head, its two large snake-like eyes, its tiny nose, large mouth, and long ears.

"Okay, I've seen enough. I can't believe this," said Susan. Without desire or volition, tears sprang from her eyes...

Instantly Roman leapt up and rushed over to her and hugged her. Had he done the right thing? Martin stood up and paced around the room.

Deactivating the TV via audio command, John said with a calm voice, "Yes it's very distressing Susan but you need to compose yourself, you need to be strong. Whenever you see them, you need to act normal. These Puppet Masters are highly intelligent... They will kill if they know you are awake."

Suddenly Martin sat back down and asked, "Why are these things here? What the hell do they want from us?"

"Martin, since the dawn of time there have always been groups that want to lead mankind, you know that. The only difference here is that these things come from another planet, and that planet is Proxima Centauri b. These aliens view us as an inferior species. They want to control us. That's it..."

Composing herself a little with Roman by her side, Susan asked, "Can these aliens reproduce?"

"Yes but only amongst themselves, alien with alien. That's what the light told me."

"I see. But tell me something, how are these aliens keeping everyone in this dream-like state? How are they keeping the masses asleep?"

"The light told me that they send out signals. These signals alter brainwave activity, neuronal activity, cognitive function, altering reality."

"These damn aliens are obviously highly advanced," snapped Martin.

"That goes without saying. They control our world. In short, human beings are living in an artificially induced state of consciousness. These aliens rule over Man because of the annihilation of consciousness. People are in a trance. The citizens of earth have become slaves to these aliens. Consciousness is a continuum that can be measured. Consciousness is not simply a binary... on or off, conscious or unconscious... but instead something that can encompass a continuum of different states that involve different kinds of brain function. For instance, consciousness can be connected to the environment through our senses and behaviour, as in most of our waking hours, or disconnected from our surroundings, as when we dream during sleep. In short, somehow these signals affect human consciousness, the brain, to the extent that these aliens appear as humans. These damn aliens are highly intelligent."

"So these signals are what keep the human race in this trance-like state?"

"Yes... correct, Martin."

"Where are these signals coming from exactly?"

Rubbing his eyes, John replied emphatically, "Machines..."

"Machines...?"

"Yes Martin, machines... In short, one machine has been placed in every country across the planet to keep the citizens of earth under this mass hypnosis. Thus these signals are constantly being spread out across our world. The good news is that once these signals are intercepted and deactivated, all the citizens of earth will see the Puppet Masters as they really are. Then a war will start."

"That's right," said Roman rubbing Susan's shoulder to comfort her.

"The important thing here to note is," snapped John, "if you deactivate one, all the others will in turn shut down. These machines operate symbiotically. Destabilize one you destabilize all, shutting them all down across the globe, thus nullifying all the signals respectively. This is what the light told me. The light then went on to tell me where the machine in the United States is located, where it's hidden. Deactivate that one and you deactivate all of them."

"Where is it then?" asked Susan who now seemed a lot calmer and composed.

"It's here in New York, hidden and operating inside the Statue of Liberty, by the head. The huge problem is that you can't get anywhere near the thing. As you all know too well it's strictly forbidden and has been for just over a century now. Once upon a time people would go to Liberty Island... tourists, etc. They would go inside the Statue of Liberty and would use the stairway or elevator to reach the top. Anyhow, if by some miracle we did find a way to get to Liberty Island safely avoiding detection and get inside the Statue of Liberty we would need to go all the way to the top. The machine is located by the head. But the truth is we will never be able to get anywhere near it. That's why it needs to be blown up from afar."

"Yes, it is constantly patrolled by the police, the military... basically the aliens!" said Roman flatly. "Soldiers are on guard on a 24-hour basis... not to mention that police-hover-jets periodically fly inspection flights around Liberty Island. On top of all of that there are surveillance cameras."

Clearing his throat John said, "In short if we blow the Statue of Liberty up from afar by targeting its head, we will destroy the machine that's hidden inside, the one that sends out the signals. It will be deactivated and that will lead to all the other machines in the world being deactivated too. The world will then slowly awaken... "

"Blow it up from afar! How? You would need a rocket launcher or something. Where are you going to get something like that from?" asked Martin.

John replied, "We need to somehow get hold of a powerful weapon. It won't be easy but that's what's needed. It's the only way."

They lapsed into silence for a while, each contemplating the enormous task ahead of them.

Rubbing his jaw, John continued... "The Statue of Liberty stands 305 feet tall for now, but it will meet its end soon. Anyway that's enough for now. I've given you plenty to chew on and we will all meet here again soon and discuss things further. We will need to find a way to get hold of a weapon. Roman, please make sure Susan and Martin have my number and my private number too."

"Yes, of course..."

"Now that your eyes have been opened," said John, his voice lowering in tone to emphasise the importance of what he was saying, "please remember what I told you. You must remain composed at all times. The aliens will kill if they know you are awake. So be careful Susan... be careful Martin. And say nothing to any one! This secret must remain strictly between us, solely. No more recruits. And please, don't worry, we will defeat these aliens... be sure about that."

Roman arrived home and Susan was with him. They decided it would be far better if she remained with him for a few days. She was still in shock.

After dropping Martin, who by that point seemed a lot calmer, at his house, they had then gone to Susan's so she could collect some clothes and basic essentials. They were now both sitting on the sofa drinking rum in the dim light of the room.

"Roman, I'm so afraid. I just can't believe it. Those faces on the TV screen... those faces walking on the streets with such arrogance..."

"I know, but don't worry... their reign is coming to an end. We know where the machine is. It will be deactivated... the Statue of Liberty destroyed. Trust me. Once we get hold of a weapon we will complete the task."

Susan rubbed her eyes, still red from tears shed, and softly said, "So these aliens came from Proxima Centauri b?"

"That's what John said. The very planet that is currently being terraformed by Man is their actual home. Bizarre, crazy even, when you think about it... The reason there are no signs of aliens up there according to reports is because they have all come here." He paused sipping his rum and then continued. "However, as I told you before, cryptic symbols and carvings have been discovered on Proxima b, indicating that an advanced long lost alien civilisation lived there. But they didn't go extinct. They are here and alive!"

After a quick, precautionary late night vid-phone call which had confirmed that his girlfriend Genevieve was human, Martin stepped out and closed the front door of his house, relieved but restless. Of course, he knew that he could not tell her anything and she had been pleased but rather bemused by his late-night call. When he'd said goodnight and promised they would see each other soon, he decided to go for a walk. It was 1:30am in the morning and bitterly cold but he knew he could not sleep given the life altering revelation he had received and he did not want to stay cooped up inside, lost in his own alarming thoughts. It would take time to digest and accept the reality that the world he thought he knew was now no more, shattered into tiny meaningless fragments by John Shackleton. He thought about his friends and wondered whether they were all human. It cut through him like a knife. Emotionally he was in tatters, his mind pulled to and thro. He was questioning everything. Suddenly in the distance he became aware of a car approaching. It was a police car.

As it got closer it pulled up beside him. Martin halted. Cold terror swept through him. He knew they were potentially dangerous. An alien stepped out looking directly at him, studying him. Martin was both fascinated and hypnotized by its face. He had to be careful.

"What are you doing out this late Sir?"

Martin melted in its presence. He tried to fight it but failed. He looked at the alien and for a moment the snake-like eyes and reptilian flesh of the alien being faded and Martin saw the flickering image of a young man. But that illusion soon dissolved away...

"Speak man. Are you drunk?" The alien inched closer realising that something was wrong. "Got some ID?"

Nervously Martin pulled out his ID card, his hand slightly trembling. He handed the card over to the alien, trying and failing to behave like a normal human being.

Looking at the card, the policeman said, "Martin McGregor, eh…?"

Martin remained silent. The alien now looked up and studied him again holding onto the card. Martin knew his eyes were filled with helpless terror and that the alien saw it too.

It said, "You better come along with me Sir."

Overcome by severe, uncontrollable panic and fear, Martin punched the alien in the face so hard it fell to the ground awkwardly and smashed its head on the concrete. Dark-green blood began to ooze from the head wound. It was motionless, dead, the ID card lying beside it. Martin knew it would breathe no more and he also knew that he had made a fatal error. Cameras were everywhere. The aliens would now suspect that he was awake, and if he was awake they would deduce that others must be too. Even if he ran he would soon be found and killed. Then eventually they would find the others… There was nowhere to go. He had let the team down. He heard the sound of a hover-car overhead and looking up he realised that it was a police-hover-car. He froze on the spot and knew with a clarity he had never felt before that his time had come. If he was captured they would force him to tell what he knew. As the hover-car pulled into position he turned and started to run. One of the aliens who was holding a laser-gun, leaned out of the side with incredible flexibility and fired.

A fiery beam of light was unleashed. It hit Martin in the back of the head and within a fraction of a second he was consumed into burning atoms, vaporized. Expertly the hover-car descended and landed on the ground. The alien who had fired stepped out and rushed over to the other alien who was lying lifelessly on the ground. It checked it over, its own kind, and soon realised it was dead.

The other alien remained seated inside the hover-car. It lowered the window and asked, "Is he still with us?"

"No," the other replied. It then noticed the ID card lying on the ground beside the body. It picked it up...

It was 10am in the morning and Roman and Susan were still on the sofa. Roman's eyes reflected his wonder and bewilderment. A numbing weight hung over him. Although the predicament of the world's situation concerning the aliens had mostly clarified in his mind, he still, at times, battled with it. Lying next to him, Susan suddenly woke up gazing towards the TV which was playing with muted volume. Slowly she got to her feet, eyes red with fatigue and fear. She stretched and yawned. Her pink wool sweater was wrinkled.

"Are you feeling better?" asked Roman softly, still wondering whether he had made the right decision. John initially did not want to tell anyone else but he had convinced him that his friends, both Susan and Martin needed to know and that it would be ultimately beneficial to them. Although he had initially thought that she could take the news concerning the aliens, he realised that it had taken a lot out of her, much more than he would have thought.

Rubbing her forehead as if sensing Roman's guilt she replied, "I'm okay. And please don't feel guilty. I needed to know, and see, see them as they really are. Had you and John succeeded in deactivating this machine I would have eventually found out anyway. And it would have been even more dramatic. Rest assured… you made the right decision." She gave him a reassuring grin.

Roman smiled, his guilt melting away. It was indeed the right thing to do. But then his attention was drawn to the TV. Martin's face was plastered across the screen. Roman was filled with horror. Susan looked at him puzzled and then turned looking at the screen. Reaching for the remote Roman raised the volume, his heart beating hard. Susan's eyes remained fixed on the screen.

The alien female news reporter said, "Terrorist **Martin McGregor** killed a police officer in the early hours of the morning during a confrontation. The officer was found on the ground bleeding heavily. Cause of death - a heavy blow to the head. Investigating officers believe that **Martin McGregor** must have pushed or punched the officer causing his injury. Thankfully, the Terrorist **Martin McGregor** was, beamed down by laser-gun by another officer before he could harm anyone else. His ID card has given police an opportunity to investigate this man's life further. It is believed that he is part of a terrorist anti-government group. If so, the others will soon be found and brought to justice. Stay tuned for updates."

"I can't believe this," exclaimed Roman looking at Susan completely distraught. He felt deeply saddened that his friend had been killed. He felt a resurgence of guilt sweep through him.

She sat next to him and tried to console him.

"Susan, I only wanted him to know so that he could be free from the hypnosis just like you, just like me. I thought we could be a team. There is strength in numbers. I thought he could take it, but I was obviously wrong. I mean, the sheer fact that he was out walking around in the early hours of the morning implies that he was struggling to deal with this."

"Oh Roman!" she commiserated, rubbing his knee gently to comfort him. "It's shocking news... this alien invasion. It's a lot to take in... Yes, the fact that Martin was out walking around in the early hours of the morning implies that he was struggling to deal with this... the aliens."

"I know..." He paused for a moment, reflecting. "In fact I did the same soon after my awakening. It was late night but I decided I needed to get out, clear my head. I even encountered a police officer on the road just as he did and it asked for my ID card. I cooperated with it and remained calm and composed saying very little avoiding any problem but poor old Martin obviously broke under pressure. He must have been questioned by the alien police officer and it must have then asked for his ID card otherwise the card would have been vaporized by the beam that ended his life. And now this has given the police, the aliens the opportunity to investigate further into his life. I should have realised, Susan. I should have insisted he came back here with us until it had sunk in properly. I've put us all in danger."

"Roman, it's not your fault. Believe me... Anyone would have wanted to share the news with their good friend. You thought he could handle it... but sadly he couldn't. You can't blame yourself."

He rubbed Susan's shoulder tenderly and replied, "Here was I feeling guilty for telling you, and now this. Once John finds out he will be deeply disappointed in me. I worked hard to convince him to recruit you and Martin and for him to awaken you both. Initially he only wanted me, but I convinced him otherwise. And now look... Beyond losing Martin, you do realise what this means, don't you? Using Martin's ID card they will start an investigation into his life, just as the alien female news reporter said. Powerful supercomputers can give so much information about individuals now with the simple click of a button. And these damn aliens are highly intelligent. Not to mention that they can track down all Martin's past movements, places he visited, friends he visited, restaurants, etc, all via his mobile phone. And he always had it with him. All his movements are recorded. It's the same for the masses. As a result they are bound to come here eventually and ask questions, and then they'll even go to John's place. Remember John is the Man from Proxima. He's high profile. Once they discover that he was at John's mansion, they may start to wonder and eventually put two and two together."

Silence fell as they both looked into each other's eyes each hoping the other had a way out of the mess they now found themselves in.

Clearing his throat, Roman eventually said, "Susan, because of what's happened with Martin, this has now become an emergency. We need to act fast. We need to find a weapon as soon as possible... somehow... in order to destroy the Statute of Liberty."

He jumped up. For a moment he felt powerless to halt events even though he knew what they had to do in order to save humanity... his family, his friends. He rushed towards the vid-phone. He needed to act fast. Composing himself he dialled. John's number and private number were both stored on the vid-phone. As the phone rang he wondered whether John had heard the news. Suddenly John's face appeared on the screen.

"John," he said almost sheepishly. "Have you heard the news?"

John remained silent; his face hard. The expression in his eyes said it all with muted clarity. Sharply aware of the fact that their call could be monitored by the authorities, he briskly and carefully replied, "Yes I have. Come and see me..."

John deactivated the call before Roman could. Roman walked back to the sofa and sat forlornly.

"Well Susan, John's heard the news alright. We'd better get ready and head to his place."

He leaned back and closed his eyes. Suddenly the doorbell rang shattering the moment. Roman's eyes sprang wide open. Susan looked at him in alarm, wondering who it was. Roman leapt to his feet and slowly approached the front door. His heart was beating fast. He peered through the small circular glass viewer in order to see who it was. His eyes popped. It was an alien dressed in a long grey coat, black shirt and a white tie. Its snake-like eyes were menacing. He had to remain calm. He turned and looked at Susan concerned how she would react.

"It's one of them," he whispered. "Go upstairs... Quick."

The doorbell rang again. Susan swiftly made her way up the stairs. Roman waited until she was out of sight and then composing himself, smoothly opened the door.

"Greetings Mr Roman Nebraska," it said with its animal-like croak pulling out a card. "I'm detective Jeff Silver. I would like to speak with you."

"Sure," replied Roman. He tried to smile but his muscles would not respond.

The alien walked over to the sofa and haughtily sat displaying the same sharp arrogance they all seemed to carry. Roman took a seat facing it.

"What brings you here detective?"

"As I'm sure you are aware, a Mr Martin McGregor had his life terminated in the early hours of this morning, around 1:40am. I believe you knew each other. Correct?"

Roman calculated fast. His mind spun. He didn't want the detective to know that he'd heard the news. It was better that way. But he would have to be honest about the fact that he knew Martin. How could he deny it? The Puppet Masters must have already tracked all Martin's movements via the phone, surveillance cameras... etc... And the plain fact that the detective was now in his house questioning him confirmed everything. It even knew his name. The Puppet Masters were experts in mind control and gaining information on all the citizens of earth at the click of a button.

Rubbing his forehead softly, he replied, "Yes, I knew Martin. But no, I hadn't heard the news. His life was terminated! Why?"

The alien's eyes widened. It replied, "Terrorist Martin McGregor killed a police officer. The officer was found on the ground bleeding heavily. Cause of death - a heavy blow to the head. Your friend Martin McGregor must have pushed or punched him, indirectly killing him. Regardless McGregor's life was terminated. And luckily we were able to retrieve his ID card. From this we have been able to dig into his life, gain lots of information. And we know that he visited here many times. We know that you were friends. Anyway, it is believed that he is part of an anti-government terrorist group. What do you have to say about that?"

Roman tried not to flinch as the alien studied his face carefully, his expression, the look in his eyes, even the small droplets of sweat that now surfaced on his cheeks.

"That's ridiculous," snapped Roman. "Martin was nothing of the sort. He was a wealthy gentleman and had a PHD in palaeontology. He loved mountain climbing... The whole notion that he was part of an anti-government terrorist group is absolutely absurd."

The alien stood up and said, "Mr Roman Nebraska I think it's best if we have your house searched." It pulled out a small communication module from its jacket. "I'm now going to contact the search team to organise the search. Once that is done, I will take you down to the police station for further questioning."

"But why...? Search the house for what? I'm a wealthy man, a paranormal investigator, explorer and freelance journalist. What do you think you'll find? And why would you want to question me further? For what...?"

"Mr Roman Nebraska you were friends with a terrorist. The implications here are vast."

"This is insane. Martin was a dear friend, a good guy. He was no terrorist. Okay he had that confrontation in the early hours of the morning with that police officer. But you can be sure that he never meant to kill him. It must have been an accident. You can be sure of that. In a moment of anger anyone can snap. Martin never meant to kill him... believe me."

"Whatever the case he is guilty of indirectly killing a law enforcement officer. As a result his life was terminated and you are implicated."

The alien turned its back as it went to activate the module in order to make the call. Roman knew that he had to act fast. If the search team came he would probably be set up. And the fact they wanted to question him further implied that they suspected he was awake. From there John would be next and their plan to save humanity would go up in smoke. Drastic action was needed. From the table Roman picked up a heavy ornament and rushed over to the alien smashing it over its head with force. The alien crashed to the floor. Dark-green blood began to ooze from the wound and its gun fell out from its jacket sliding across the marble floor. Dropping the ornament, Roman rushed over and picked up the gun. The alien, still dimly alert, got to its feet swaying back and forth.

It said, "You can see us, can't you?"

"Yes, I can see you, and your reign is coming to an end."

Staggering around, fighting for life, the alien replied, its snake-like eyes filled with anger, "Never... You will never..."

Roman raised the gun and fired. The alien stopped in mid-sentence and fell to the ground dead. He stood near it and said, imitating the alien croak, "You can see us, can't you?" He paused smirking and in his own voice now said, "Yes you're damn right about that..." Composing himself he now knew that he had to act fast. Time was against them... But how would they get hold of a weapon that would destroy the Statue and the machine so quickly?

"Susan, quick come down, it's safe," he called, hoarse with adrenaline.

Susan quickly made her way down the stairs and rushed over to the lifeless body of the alien. Pressing her fingers to her lips she gazed up at Roman and gasped feebly, "You've killed it."

"I had no choice." He paused as he contemplated what he had done.

Susan shuddered with fear and despair.

"Let's get ready and get out of here. We should head to John's place. Somehow we need to find a weapon as soon as possible. That Statue needs to come down by tonight otherwise we are all doomed. We have little time, especially now... They will soon come here looking for their detective. Then all hell will break loose."

He rushed into the bathroom. He was exhausted, riddled with fatigue. His body ached. But he had to keep going. He filled the bowl with hot water, rolled up his sleeves and washed his face and hands in the swirling hot water. Briefly he glanced up and looked into the mirror. It was a terrified reflection; trembling mouth, pulse-fluttering throat. Regardless of the pain and mental torture it was time to move on and accomplish the seemingly impossible mission.

Roman and Susan had just arrived. They were in the living room sitting on the now familiar sofa along with Alexanko. They were all waiting for John. He was in his bedroom getting dressed. In the silence Susan nervously reached for a book that was on the table. Subconsciously she was trying to escape the situation. Suddenly John entered the living room and she fumbled the book and it fell to the floor. He was dressed in black trousers and a dark blue coat. Susan retrieved the book and placed it on the table. Without wasting anytime, John got straight to the point.

"Roman my decision to listen to you has backfired with devastating consequences. We should have stuck to the original plan. Martin's face has been all over the news. His story has already been told a thousand times... He's now known as a terrorist, an anti-government police killer. Of course only they could create such lies. They know, or at least suspect, that he was awake and will conclude that there must be others." Seconds of weighted silence passed... John continued... "Via his phone, surveillance cameras, etc, they will now track all his past movements. They will gather all the information they need and eventually that will lead them to us..."

"Yes," Roman interjected dejectedly, "It has already happened."

"What do you mean?"

"A little while after speaking with you on the vid-phone a certain detective named Jeff Silver, an alien, paid me a visit. Susan went upstairs and I dealt with it as needed."

"Did you kill it?"

"Yes, I had no choice. It wanted my house searched. It was about to call the search team to organise everything. Once organised, it wanted to take me down to the police station for further questioning. I had no choice but to kill it."

John rubbed his eyes and said, "That's it. We all need to get out of here as soon as possible. This has made matters even worse. Martin's death was one thing, this is another. When the alien detective fails to reply to calls and doesn't return to the police station with you they will send officers to your house and then all hell will break loose... Your face will soon be on the television all over the news just like Martin's. Only you are still alive, thus... a wanted man... a terrorist, a killer, who needs to be stopped at all costs."

"So what's the plan now?" asked Roman... "The Statue needs to come down by tonight... We have very little time. How are we going to get hold of a weapon in the next few hours?"

"We can't. We don't have enough time. It's impossible. Getting a weapon for such a task will take time. But I have another plan that will work just as affectively."

"What do you mean exactly?"

"Given the desperate circumstances which we now all face, I know exactly what needs to be done Roman." John's eyes grew wide. "And I will tell you in due course. Trust me. Come... let's go."

They were flying smoothly high above the city of New York. Gliding gently through the atmosphere gave them all a sense of comfort and protection. They were detached from the world, nestled inside this hover car while the masses remained hypnotised by the Puppet Masters below. Roman was seated in the front whilst John piloted. On the back seats both Susan and Alexanko sat in silence. John increased altitude and then stabilised the hover car. The metallic silver coloured vehicle was unusually spacious. The control panel was bright.

"Okay John, you've kept us waiting long enough. Can you tell us how you are planning to destroy the Statue of Liberty from afar without a weapon?" asked Roman anxiously.

John pointed down and said, "Look there's the Statue standing 305 feet tall... 31 tons of copper and 125 tons of steel."

Out in the distance they could all see the Statue, Liberty Island, and the old Museum. As always it was heavily patrolled by the military, the aliens.

"Roman, in answer to your question, the only available weapon that we have at the moment is this hover car..."

Roman turned his head and looked at John, his eyes wide, face blank as if starved of energy. He was speechless. He was shocked.

"Roman, I'm going to fly this hover car straight into the Statue of Liberty, targeting the head. A direct impact with this hover car will cause an explosion destroying the Statue's shell and the machine inside. Job done! Task accomplished... I will breathe my last but there is no other way. Once it gets dark I'm going in alone. It will be easier for me to approach Liberty Island in the gloom of night somewhat concealed by the darkness. As I mentioned before to you, it's just a load of copper castings attached to the steel framework. The Statue's copper shell, its skin, will perish along with the machine inside once this hover car crashes into it at a high velocity."

For a moment there was stunned silence. Roman rubbed his forehead. There was nothing more to say at this point. He knew it was the only way to put an end to the alien invasion and deactivate the machine which was hidden inside. It was sad but there were no other options. Someone had to die, and it would be John, the legend, the Man from Proxima. He pictured it, it was locked in his mind, and the image hardened to reality.

Fiddling with a dial, John then said, "The Man from Proxima is going to sacrifice his life to save the world. We have very little time left. You can be sure that they have already found the dead alien in your house. And I'm sure that they have already swarmed my mansion looking for you... us. They would have put two and two together. These Puppet Masters work quickly and are highly intelligent. Just as with Martin, they would have monitored all your movements via your phone, surveillance cameras, etc, which would then, lead them to me at the mansion." He paused... Clearing his throat he then said, "That light revealed everything to me, and it gave me the power to make others see, and now I will put an end to this alien invasion... I feel compelled to do so. I feel like I was chosen. I will be a martyr. But my death will awaken the masses setting Mankind free at last..."

"I'm coming with you," snapped Alexanko bravely, tears gathering in the corners of his eyes. "Together till the end..."

"As you wish my dear friend..."

Seconds of silence fell... hearts beating fast.

"As for you Roman, Susan," he said softly, "I will leave you somewhere safe... relativity speaking of course. You will both get to see the resulting war unfold and I truly hope that you both survive the ordeal."

Roman sat in silence, his mind spinning. There was nothing more to say. The matter was settled.

Earth tilted toward nine o'clock. They had circled the city for hours, silent, gliding through the atmosphere, eating up time. Darkness had descended and the city of New York below now appeared as an endless cluster of luminous flickering dots. Their eyes had accustomed to the night gloom. Above Roman could see the faint sheen of starlight... the lonely emptiness between the stars... the unreverberant abyss through which a man could fall until the end of time... space.

"Right the hour has come," said John definitively.

ANTONY FUCILLA

With expert fingers he manipulated controls and fiddled with dials. It was all bathed in light. The hover car started to descend. Slowly the city below started to take shape and form as they got closer to the ground. Eventually they landed softly beside a towering line of skyscrapers. John thought that this would be a safe place to leave Roman and Susan. No aliens were in sight.

"Roman, Susan it's time for you to both leave my friends," he said calmly.

Across the street was an oriental bar called SNAKE. Its bright sign flashed green. Music was playing, dimly audible. A few human faces were visible sitting inside the bar drinking and chatting. Ahead, bright neon signs glowed in the gloom. A lumbering delivery truck, now empty, clattered off down the street disappearing into the distance. The warm odour of cooking drifted through the air.

Roman turned peering into Susan's eyes and said, "See that bar, SNAKE? Go in there and wait for me. I won't be long."

"Please hurry," she replied softly, her eyes burning with fear. She was also saddened by the fact that both John and Alexanko were about to die even if it was for the greater good.

John sensing her sadness turned and looked at her. "Don't worry Susan. This alien invasion ends tonight."

Alexanko carefully opened the back door and stepped out looking around. Still no aliens were in sight. He wanted to say goodbye to Susan. She stepped out from the opening and stood staring at him mute and fearful.

Although she barely knew him, a bond had formed. After all they were the only people on the planet along with John and Roman that could see the aliens as they really were.

"Stay strong Susan. Remember the world is about to awaken."

He hugged her knowing that his life would soon come to an end. Pulling away from him she smiled and then dashed towards the bar. As Susan entered a big heavy-set man, middle aged, with red hair and beer-swollen features suddenly lurched out. 'It seems safe enough in there for now,' thought Roman, getting ready to leave the hover car. He knew that he would soon be with her. He opened the door. Another truck passed, rumbling under its tightly packed load. As a frigid wind blew, Alexanko turned to make his way back inside the hover car. The night was ice chill. But suddenly from seemingly out of nowhere two alien police officers appeared in the moth-ridden darkness of night. Alexanko saw them and for a brief moment was paralyzed by fear.

"The aliens are here," he yelled in desperation.

Both Roman and John turned around and saw them, wary and alert. Before Alexanko had time to get back inside one of the officers shot him in the back and he fell to the ground dead.

"Freeze," shouted the other pointing the gun at the hover car.

"Quick, ascend," yelled Roman, pulling the door closed. "They've killed Alexanko…"

With expert fingers John ascended rapidly with the back door still open, cold air sweeping in. The sudden ascension made them feel sick. The alien officers now both fired at the moving hover car, but their bullets were useless. The hover car was bullet proof, the windows too. As they ascended somewhat wildly, Roman realised that he wasn't going to be able to meet Susan in the bar as planned. He was now imprisoned within the hover car. The sudden appearance of the two alien cops had ruined the plan entirely. He also wondered anxiously whether they had seen her entering the bar. He gazed into the night sky trying to summon courage, breathing in deeply... his mind spinning.

"These damn aliens have killed Martin and now Alexanko too," snapped Roman.

"Yes, but their reign is about to come to an end," replied John calmly as he manoeuvred the hover car.

Before they knew it they were flying over the sea, the cold waters of the Atlantic, heading in the direction of Liberty Island. Suddenly police-hover-jets appeared behind them in the distance, their lights flashing, pulsing red and green in the night darkness. The shrill shrieks of sirens thundered everywhere. Down below on Liberty Island alien soldiers began shouting, yelling and firing bullets. A violent alarm shrilled loudly. In a growing panic, Roman wondered how he would exit the hover car safely before impact and began to contemplate the unpalatable truth that he was going to accompany John into oblivion. Suddenly the hover car descended hurtling towards the sea. As it got closer John reduced velocity.

"Jump and swim for it my friend. Quick..."

Bracing himself and in the panic of the moment not even looking back, he opened the door and jumped out, falling feet first into the sea. He plunged deep down into the water but quickly resurfaced unharmed. He watched the hover car ascending to an altitude that would see it crash directly into the head of the Statue of Liberty destroying the machine inside.

John increased the velocity to the max as more bullets hit the hover car with no effect. The police-hover-jets that were behind him were getting closer by the second but it was futile. The chill of death touched him. John the legend, the Man from Proxima as he was known to all, closed his eyes.

Treading water, trying to ignore the bone-chilling cold, Roman watched as the hover car reached Liberty Island and crashed directly into the head of the Statue of Liberty blowing its copper shell apart and destroying the machine inside. Fire raged. Smoke ascended into the dark atmosphere. The alien soldiers on guard all ran towards the boats in terror and defeat, trying to avoid falling debris and burning detritus. The flames lit up the night sky in a glorious display. Roman witnessed it all, watching the police-hover-jets now circling above Liberty Island. The internal steel framework remained intact, but the Statue's copper shell was destroyed... the head blown away along with the machine itself. It had finally been deactivated, nullifying all signals. And all the other machines in turn would be symbiotically deactivated globally. Roman was not sure if he could reach the shore, but it was better to try rather than just sink below the icy surface. He set out with a strong steady rhythm that only faltered when the sounds of screaming and chaos reached his ears, carried across the harbour on a gentle breeze.

The city of New York did awake for the very first time, so too the entire planet as all signals deactivated across the globe. Mankind had finally been set free from the mass hypnosis. The war began... Many perished on both sides but the victory ultimately belonged to humanity. Both Roman and Susan lived to see the victory that finally came. The few remaining aliens who had survived the brutal battle left the planet in a spaceship heading into deep space. The citizens of earth were now free from the dominance and rule of the Puppet Masters.

TIME elapsed...

A huge shadow swept overhead. Beneath the perpetually shining red dwarf, down on the surface of Proxima Centauri b, engineer Miroslav Boniek looked up. His eyes filled with terror as an alien spaceship began to descend towards the ground...

www.ingramcontent.com/pod-product-compliance
Lightning Source LLC
Chambersburg PA
CBHW070828250626
47170CB00006B/2245